Lace-Covered
COMPROMISE

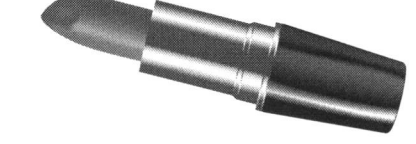

SILVIA VIOLET

RIPTIDE
PUBLISHING

Riptide Publishing
PO Box 1537
Burnsville, NC 28714
www.riptidepublishing.com

Lace-Covered Compromise

Cover art: L.C. Chase, lcchase.com/design.htm
Editor: Carole-ann Galloway
Layout: L.C. Chase, lcchase.com/design.htm

ISBN: 978-1-62649-685-9

First edition
November, 2017

Also available in ebook:
ISBN: 978-1-62649-658-3

Lace-Covered COMPROMISE

SILVIA VIOLET

RIPTIDE
PUBLISHING

To friends and family who've always supported my career and given me the love and encouragement to keep writing.

Table of CONTENTS

Chapter
ONE

I watched as my father's coffin was lowered into the ground. Most of the other funeral goers had left, including Nate, the self-righteous prick who now owned half of Kingston Corp., the company my father had built from the ground up.

It was supposed to be mine. All mine. Not split up with someone who isn't family, no matter how convinced he was that Nate would run it better.

The few mourners—was anyone other than Nate actually mourning or had they just shown up in hopes of making the papers?—had moved far away, standing in darkly-clad clusters, whispering, perhaps sharing their most damning memories of my father. How many of them had happy reminiscences? Mine were sure as hell few and far between.

"Sir, do you need a moment?"

It took me a bit to realize the funeral director was speaking to me. I shook my head. "Go ahead and put the old bastard under."

The man nodded, his face remaining impressively blank. He must hear all kinds of sentiments in his business. I turned and walked away, scanning the paths to see if I could escape the cemetery without talking to anyone. Not fucking likely if I went back the way I'd come in. Fortunately, I didn't have to. At least I'd made it through the ceremony without one of the fucking panic attacks I'd been having recently. Yet another thing I had to thank dear old Dad for.

I pulled out my phone. "Darryl, bring the car to the south entrance. I'll meet you there."

My aunt and my wicked ex-stepmother had assigned themselves as my keepers during this blessed event. They'd done their best to parade me in front of all the attending media, but now it was time to make my escape. I headed where there seemed to be no funeral goers or photographers hoping for another shot of the grieving son. As if. There were probably a few members of the press hiding somewhere, but at least they were discreet. What had my stepmother thought I was going to do, anyway? Stand up in front of everyone and say how I really felt? I might've done so if I'd thought anyone would actually care, but I'd had enough of being a scandalmonger for a while.

In his last hours, my father had pretended to reach out to me, to forgive past mistakes—in other words, he'd given me a chance to apologize for being a disappointment. I'd wanted to believe he was sincere, but no, Daddy had put a nice little surprise for me in his will. He'd probably laughed behind my back every time I visited during his final illness.

"Adam! Adam!"

I ignored the female voice calling me. It would be best for everyone if I got out of there without having to speak to another person.

"Adam!"

Wait. Was that Valerie? She wasn't supposed to be here yet.

I turned and there she stood, the woman my father had wanted me to marry. He'd tried to set plans in motion when I was still in high school, but we'd known we'd make a lousy match, so instead of becoming engaged, we became best friends. Valerie understood what it was like to live with parents who wanted to mold you in their image.

Now, we saw each other as often as we could even though she lived in the tiny principality of Nazapoli near the Italian Alps. She'd fallen madly in love with actual Nazapolitan royalty and become a duchess with lots of important state duties.

"You're here." Obviously she was or else I was worse off than I thought.

She nodded. "I am."

"But I didn't think you were going to make it for the funeral."

"My pilot was able to take off early."

"Ah, yes, being connected to a royal family does have its advantages."

"It does." Valerie pulled me into her arms. I was so startled I let her, though normally—unless I was fucking somebody—I liked to keep people at arm's length.

When she pulled back, I scowled at her.

"I needed the hug even if you didn't," she said.

"Selfish brat."

"Pot. Kettle."

I smiled for the first time that day. Almost a year had passed since I'd seen Valerie, but she was as beautiful as ever. She wore a perfectly tailored black sheath dress, and her dark hair was swirled up in an impeccable Audrey Hepburn–esque style. She could easily have walked off the set of an early 1960s film. I was surprised photographers hadn't mobbed her.

Valerie took my hands in hers, and because she was my best friend, I allowed that too. "How are you? And don't give me any bullshit."

"Pissed off."

She nodded. "That sounds right."

"You're not even going to pretend to be shocked that I'm not grief-stricken?"

"I've never pretended with you, Adam, and I appreciate that you don't pretend with me, either."

That was true. No matter how tempting it would've been to get my father off my back, I never pretended I might marry her.

"I couldn't get this day over with fast enough. The old ass should consider himself lucky I showed up at all." I offered her my arm, and we started walking the way I'd been headed. "Thank you for letting me be honest."

"So the rumor is true, I take it?" she asked.

I snorted. She had to be referring to my father fucking me over on my inheritance. "How much time do you have?"

"As much as you need. I'll be in Chicago for a month, and I don't have any plans tonight. But if I did, I'd cancel for you."

"I asked my driver to circle to the back of the cemetery. Would you like to get a drink?"

"I would love that, but I think we'd better go back to your apartment or my hotel if we don't want to be surrounded." She tilted her head toward a photographer who was literally hiding behind a tree watching us.

"Fuck off," I yelled.

"Adam." She batted my arm.

"Now you're pretending. Nothing I do really shocks you."

"I'm simply attempting to correct your abysmal manners."

I snorted. "I suppose you've always done that."

"Sadly, I've always needed to."

"You'd do best to give up on trying to teach me propriety; even my father eventually did." I stumbled on the uneven pavement, surprised by the pain of the memories that confession brought up. The one thing I never wanted to do was fail, yet my father had thought I was a failure at basically everything.

"Hang on just a minute. Let me call my driver." By the time she'd finished telling her own driver that he wouldn't be needed, we'd reached my car.

"Where to, Mr. Kingston?" Darryl asked.

"My apartment."

"Yes, sir."

"At least then I won't be seen going to a married woman's hotel room," I said, when I was seated next to Valerie on the soft leather seat.

"No, just taking one up to your flat."

I gave her a mocking, wide-eyed glance. "Surely no one would think I'd seduce an old friend on the day of my father's funeral."

"That is exactly the kind of thing you'd do."

"Too true, but . . ." I gestured toward the diamond on her left hand, which was so large her husband could probably see it all the way across the Atlantic. "I don't do married women."

She scoffed. "Nice to know there's something you don't do. Now tell me about your father and the very attractive man who now owns half of Kingston Corp."

I opened the limousine's liquor cabinet and poured myself a Scotch. "Would you like a drink?" I asked, glancing at Valerie.

"No, thank you. One of us should be sober."

"That's sure as hell not going to be me." I downed my drink and poured another. I sipped this one for a few moments and then felt ready to talk. "To answer your question, yes, the rumor is right.

Fucking Nate fucking Thomas now owns half of Kingston Corp. Half. Of. My. Company. The nerdy little tree-hugging enviro-nut who wants to turn the all of Kingston Corp. into some kind of pro-Earth charity now owns half of it, and I've got to figure out how to overturn the will or get him to sell. Maybe I can convince him it's evil to own the means of production or something."

"I doubt he's truly a communist—are there still communists? From what I've read about him, he seems like an idealist and certainly pro-environment, but—"

"You haven't met the self-smug bastard."

"I'm going to make a wild guess here, based on everything I know about Adam Kingston. Is the real problem that he hates you and refuses to do what you say?"

"He . . . Yes." Why could Valerie always read me like that?

Valerie tucked in a piece of hair that had escaped from its confines. "This should prove interesting."

"I don't want it to be interesting. I want it to be over."

"Have you ever actually talked to Nate?"

I glared at her.

"Well, have you?"

"We're at every division president's meeting together. Most weeks, he tells me I'm callous and reckless, and I argue that he's trying to give all our profits away. He makes me lose my temper faster than anyone other than my father."

"Telling him how wrong he is isn't talking to him."

"We have discussions, they are just—"

Valerie raised her brows. "Do you, or do you dictate and expect him to obey?"

"I . . . Fuck, why do you always have to act like things are my fault? That is one reason I could never marry you."

"One of a billion reasons. Do you have another one to confess?"

The gleam in her eye made it clear she had something specific in mind, but she knew most of the reasons, except . . . Fuck, had she figured out that I liked men? I'd never even hinted at it, and it wasn't a reason for not marrying her. I liked women too.

Someone must know. You can't truly believe you've kept it secret all these years.

One day I would get caught with a man and more people than my father would lose respect for me. But until then, the adrenaline of almost getting caught on a regular basis only made my dirty secret better.

"What is that look about?" Valerie asked.

"Nothing."

"It's never nothing with you."

"Why do I feel like I'm twenty again with you trying to get me to take something, anything, seriously?"

"Because neither of us has really changed."

I smiled. "What the fuck am I going to do about Nate?"

"You're going to have to talk to him and work this out like an adult, one qualified to run a global conglomerate."

I hated how right she was.

Chapter
TWO

The fucking will turned out to be airtight. After a week, my lawyers couldn't find a single loophole, and I'd hired the best. The problem was, so had my dad. Apparently, my father could give the company to anyone he chose. There was no chance of proving that my old man wasn't in his right mind when he wrote the will. He'd been as sane as ever. Shrewd, unfeeling, vengeful, but sane.

I was going to have to talk to Nate or, as Valerie would put it, talk at Nate and hope he'd listen. There wasn't much chance of that, though. He might be a woolly headed, put-the-world-ahead-of-profit hippie, but he was smart—not as smart as me, but damn close. And he was stubborn, really fucking stubborn.

And you're not?

My father had taught us both to never relent. I couldn't understand his interest in Nate. Not long after hiring him, my father had taken Nate under his wing. Over the years, he'd spent more and more time acting as a mentor, but from what I could see, Nate was less like my father's ideal son than I was. My father had been a smooth-talking businessman who'd seduced companies into rolling over and showing their belly. Then, when they were too weak to fight, he'd take control, buying them out and merging them into Kingston. I'd always thought my dad wanted a fox for a son, a fox in bunny's clothing. I was ruthless, but I didn't have the patience for the sweet talk or seduction. I didn't wait for an opponent to show weakness, I just went right for the kill, like a shark.

Nate thought you could succeed in business by making everyone happy. He sincerely believed he could make the world a better place.

The fool. So how the fuck had he been my father's protégé? No way in hell had he actually converted my old man to his way of thinking. Harvey Kingston had never changed his mind, not for any man, woman, or child other than my mother, but she'd been gone so long he'd forgotten how to bend.

I glanced at the time on my laptop screen. Nate would be out of his meeting with my father's attorneys. I could head down to his office and catch him off guard. Beard him in his den, as it were. It was time he understood that it was my place to decide the direction this company would go. He'd simply have to get on board.

Nate understood environmental science, and I agreed with my father's decision to put him in charge of the Enviro division. I might even be able to stomach letting him run the division however he wanted to, but the future of Kingston Corp. depended on me putting plans into action in the Research division, plans he might not like. The board wanted us to share leadership with me as CEO and Nate as president, a position we would create just for him. No way in hell was that going to work. I doubted he'd even been keeping up with Kingston's financial reports, and he'd likely fallen for my father's bullshit about how bright the future looked. My father had insisted nothing was wrong up until the day he died, but Kingston was in serious financial trouble, and I needed to get us back on track.

I had a few ideas about how to do that, one of which was to reduce Kingston's reach. My father had originally started Kingston Corp. as a household products company, but as the world and the market had shifted, Kingston had become a conglomerate, owning and overseeing a number of diverse businesses. As much as I hated the thought of selling off any of those divisions, I would do what was necessary. Because, despite what my father thought, failure wasn't an option for me.

The elevator dinged. I'd reached Nate's floors. As the doors glided open, I stepped into the Enviro business's executive offices. As I walked through the sea of cubicles, I heard a wave of whispers cross the floor. Apparently one girl thought I might be planning to finish Nate off. I wasn't quite that ruthless. This wasn't the Old West. Hell, we weren't even in Texas. Although there was some appeal to the idea of settling this all with a duel. I'd rather be shot at than spend hours, days, weeks negotiating with someone who didn't understand profit margins.

Nate's assistant, Michelle, was at her desk, but I blew past her and pushed his office door open so hard it banged against the wall. His back was to me, and he jumped, knocking a gym bag off the chair in front of him. He must have been putting something in it, because it was unzipped and the contents spilled onto the floor. He grabbed the bag and started frantically shoving everything inside. *What the fuck? His smelly gym shorts can't be that different than—* Oh my fucking God. I caught a glimpse of pink lace. I might've thought he'd hooked up with some girl at the gym except Nate didn't go for girls, which meant . . . No way. He didn't . . .

He zipped the bag and tossed it to the side of the room where it knocked over a stack of papers. I couldn't stop staring at it. Those were lace panties. Nate's lace panties? Oh my God.

Finally I tore my gaze away, but Nate was looking out the window, so I glanced around his office, determined I wouldn't look at the gym bag. Wow. The office was a mess. My father would've hated it. I started counting the number of seltzer cans Nate had stacked on a shelf.

Nate turned around and I looked up. He held my gaze as if daring me to mention what I'd seen, his cheeks pink with embarrassment.

Normally I took every chance I could to taunt him, but this time I was too busy trying to understand my own reaction. I couldn't seem to think—all my blood had rushed to my cock. Another one of the damnable things about Nate was that despite being so unaffected and nerdy and probably wearing pants made of hemp cloth, he was fucking hot. His arms might've been the most perfectly formed ones I'd ever seen, and his ass . . . I couldn't stop thinking of it covered in pink lace. I'd never, not even in my most secret dirty jerk-off fantasies, gotten off on a man wearing lingerie. I didn't usually like feminine men, much less men in something as ridiculous as manties, but Nate. In fucking pink lace. Holy shit, that was going to be my new favorite thing.

No, no, I was going to block it from my mind, unless it became useful in the near future. It was always good to know someone's secrets. Someone's hot, dirty secret.

Now what the fuck was I doing in his office?

Nate cleared his throat. "I'm assuming you're here about the will," he said, his tone measured.

My anger came rushing back. "Of course I'm here about the will." My father had fucked over my entire future by giving half my company to Nate. I certainly wasn't here to chat with him about the weather.

"I suppose you think you have some 'solution' to this 'problem.'"

If only I could knock the smug look right off his face, if only I didn't find him so goddamned intriguing. "I know I do."

"One that involves me backing down on everything I believe in."

I pretended to consider his words. "Not everything."

"If we're going to discuss this, let's take a walk." He looked down as he closed a folder that was open on his desk. His blond hair fell over his forehead; his bangs were far too long for his professional status. I bet if he weren't in an executive position, he'd wear his hair long, put it up in a fucking man bun or one of those little ponytails that might be hot on a guy at a club, but not in the fucking office. No, definitely not. I would have no interest in yanking his hair down and running my hands through it. Fuck no.

"You want us to take a walk?"

"Yes. You know, exercise and take in some of the air I want to make fresher. You do go outside on occasion, right?"

I scowled at him. "When I have to."

Silently, we walked to Wacker and strolled along the river. Finally Nate said, "I'm assuming you want me to hand over control, run Enviro, and keep my mouth shut?"

Well, he certainly knew me. "Well, I—"

"Or do you just want me to quit altogether, saying I don't want to take part in owning an evil corporation?"

Could he read my fucking mind? "The first one seems more realistic."

"Yeah . . . no. That's not how this is going to go."

I fisted my hands, fighting the urge not to yell. "It would be easier."

"For you."

"For both of us. Do you really want to spend every day arguing with me?"

He sighed. "If that's what it takes."

"I won't back down." *Not even when anxiety has me in a stranglehold.* Kingston was all I had, and I wouldn't lose it.

"I'd much rather try to make a difference than spend so much time arguing," Nate said. "You could help me do that, Adam. We don't have to focus all our energy on profit."

"Yes, we do." While a part of me wondered what it would be like to ride his energy and enthusiasm, I had to prove my father wrong, show him I could run things my way.

"Don't you care about anything else?" His words jabbed at me.

"I care about keeping this company going."

"Don't you have enough money already?" he shouted.

Wow! I'd actually made Nate Thomas yell in public.

Nate glanced around uneasily. His outburst had turned heads. Someone would recognize me soon or even him. Dad had seen to putting his face out there enough. *God knows it's a face you could sell things with. Fucking gorgeous asshole.*

"My father may not have been completely honest with you about the state of things at Kingston."

"Can't you wait until he's been dead a few months before you start in on how terrible he was?"

"Oh, did I forget to look that up in my etiquette guide? Is there a set amount of time to wait before telling it like it is? Some people are fuckers; my dad was one. Being dead doesn't change that."

"God, Adam, you really didn't know him at all."

"Maybe it's you who didn't know him." Now I was the one who was yelling. I was also contemplating pushing his pious ass in the river.

Nate spun around and started walking back toward Kingston.

"Walk's over then? Did I get enough of the not-very-fresh air?"

"You're in no frame of mind to listen to me." He rubbed at his forehead. Maybe I'd given him a headache. I sure as hell had one.

"And I'm never going to be."

"Which is why this isn't going to work."

"So you're ready to step down?"

"No, I'm going to fight, but if we can't come to a compromise, we'll tear this company apart."

The fucker was right. If we didn't get a plan into action soon, things would disintegrate because we were sailing for the edge of the cliff as it was. Nate just didn't know it. All he knew was Enviro, which was part of why having him in charge of the whole company was absurd.

"Let me know when you're ready to listen," Nate said. "But don't wait too long. The company won't run itself."

He stomped off in the direction of Kingston. So much for mild-mannered. The sassy little shit.

You like sassy little shits.

I did, but liking Nate was very inconvenient, so I ignored that thought and celebrated the fact that I'd gotten to him, because sometimes I really was the bastard most people thought I was.

My celebration was short-lived, though. I was going to have to figure out how to work with him. As much as I hated to admit it, Enviro made money and the profits were needed to bolster the rest of the company. Instead of following him back to Kingston, I sat on a bench and wrote him an email, adding links to the encrypted files that would show him just how bad things were. Hopefully after meeting with the lawyers today, Nate had his all-access pass to everything Kingston Corp. My father would've made sure the transfer was taken care of swiftly. He wouldn't want me to be the only one with the keys to the *King*-dom, especially since he'd never given me full access when he was alive. *Shitfaced fucker.* Fortunately, hacking had been my teenage deviant behavior of choice. My father had never realized I was privy to all his private dealings.

After I hit Send, I slipped my phone into my pocket and started walking again, away from Kingston. I considered keeping on going, taking a train to the airport, and flying off somewhere. Maybe Kingston was too much trouble and Nate should just have it. But how and where would I start over? Most people would enjoy lying on a beach doing fuck all. I had the money to sustain that lifestyle for quite some time, but I would be restless before a day was up. I didn't do idle well.

I was, in fact, a control freak, and I needed things done my way, but I'd built Kingston's Research division into something I was damn proud of. I couldn't let my father's stupid investment ruin everything I'd worked for.

I stopped at a hot dog cart and ordered myself a traditional Chicago dog and a Coke. Then I sat on a bench enjoying the fatty meat. Hot dogs were truly one of life's simple pleasures. I tried to imagine Nate joining me, but he was probably a fucking vegetarian, maybe even a vegan. If so, he didn't know what he was missing. Surely eating some meat wouldn't wreck his fucking perfect physique, with his goddamn broad shoulders and arms that strained the sleeves of his dress shirt.

An image of him popped into my head but he wasn't wearing a suit any more. He was in pink lace panties, all worked up, preaching his make-the-world-better rhetoric while wearing pink lace.

Did he truly wear the scrap of lace I'd seen in his hand? Maybe they belonged to a boyfriend? But my mind refused to believe that and I had to shift on the bench as my cock started to respond to the images in his head.

Think of something else.
Like what?
Anything.

I imagined packing up my office because Kingston had gone under. That did it.

I stuffed the last bite of hot dog in my mouth, stood, and tossed the wrapper in the trash. I believed in keeping Chicago clean, and honestly, I was on board with most of what Nate cared about. I just hated when people were so fucking sanctimonious about their causes, trying to make you feel guilty for every little misstep.

I wasn't going to back down. I would get my way with Kingston, and Nate would simply have to accept it.

Chapter THREE

"Why didn't you tell me how things stood?" Nate demanded.

He'd burst into my office just as I was packing up to head home—or more likely to my favorite bar to get really fucking drunk. "I was going to, but you took exception to me disparaging my poor dead father."

Nate closed his eyes and exhaled audibly. "I looked through the records to see where you'd found those files. I didn't see them anywhere. How did you get them?"

"They're encrypted. Daddy didn't want anyone to see them."

"And of course you can break the encryption."

I smiled. "I can break anything given time."

"This is serious."

"Fuck yes, it is. That's why I—"

"Stop!"

We glared at each other for several moments and time seemed to stretch. Then Nate sighed and stepped back. "There's no point in continuing to argue. Why don't I make a plan and you make a plan and we'll both present them to the board?"

"What, and they'll pick between us, like it's a contest?"

Nate shrugged. "Or we can find a compromise."

Like that was going to happen. What if I agreed to this and then I lost? No, that wasn't an option. I didn't lose. Besides, I knew the board way better than he did.

"So if the board likes my proposal best, you'll go along with it?" I asked.

"How far down the road will this plan get us?"

How evasive could I be? "Far enough to get us out of the hole we're in."

Nate considered for a few seconds and then nodded. "Yes, if you'll agree to the same terms."

"That I'll accept your plan if the board does?"

"That's right."

How bad of a risk was this? What else could I do? Bend him to my will? Strangle him? I considered the last for a few seconds, staring at his neck at the way it curved, his collarbone, and . . . *Oh, fuck. Please let him not have noticed.*

When I looked up, he was smirking at me.

Goddamn fuck.

"Yes?" he asked, his tone smug. He had to know how fucking hot he was, though his looks always seemed so unstudied.

Not that I was sympathizing with him or anything. "I agree to your terms."

"Seriously?"

"Are you suggesting I would be unreasonable about such a thing?" He gave a bitter laugh and turned to leave. He had his messenger bag with him. "Are you going home?"

"Yes."

"The board meeting's tomorrow night. How quickly do you think you can come up with a plan to save the company?"

"I'm going out tonight."

Immediately my brain—the fucking traitor—conjured up an image of him in panties with his legs wrapped around another man. "You . . . have . . .?" My mind had ceased to work.

I hated how easily my thoughts of him could turn from anger to lust. Maybe I should've strangled him earlier. I glanced around the office. If I did it now, was there a way to dispose of the body? His gorgeous body that I wanted so badly.

No, I wasn't supposed to like him, to wonder if he'd focus as intently on a lover as he did on whoever was speaking to him in a meeting. My infatuation with him was getting out of control. My chest tightened and the edges of my vision darkened. Shit! This was no time for a panic attack. I took a long slow breath. *I'm okay. I'm okay.*

"Are you okay?" he asked. The tenderness in his voice wasn't making this easier.

"Yes." I paused for another slow breath. "I'm fine. More than fine since it looks like you're basically handing this to me." When in doubt, fall back on being an asshole.

"I already have a plan to give the company a new direction. I created it weeks ago. I just need to tweak it to deal with the current crisis."

Fucking asshole. I slapped my hand down on my desk. "You knew what my father had planned. You knew he'd give you part ownership."

"I suspected it, but that doesn't matter. All you have to do is come up with something better. You've still got—" He glanced at his watch. "—twenty-five hours. A genius like you should be able to beat me in half that time."

"Get the fuck out of my office." I was never going to think he was too nice again.

He gave me one last smirk and left.

Later that evening, I paced my living room, looking out at the city. How the hell was I going to outdo Nate with my plan to get Kingston out of this mess? I needed a bold plan, something Nate would never attempt.

I needed someone to brainstorm with, so I grabbed the phone and called Valerie. I'd thought it would be best to give her a night on her own since the media was convinced we were having an affair—she kept texting me links to articles with headlines like: *Now That She's Taken, Kingston Wants Her* and *The Duchess and the King-ston*—but I needed her.

"I need to bounce some ideas off you," I said when she answered.

"What are you up to now?" Valerie asked.

"I've got to develop a better plan than Nate's, a much better plan, one the board members will eat up but which accomplishes most of my goals. See, I can compromise."

She rolled her eyes. "As long as it's only with yourself."

"It's not my fault I'm always right."

She laughed. "You really haven't changed a bit. Should I come over?"

"Yes." I glanced around at the mess of papers. "No. Oh fuck, I don't know what I'm going to do."

"I'll be there in less than an hour."

I hadn't made any progress when she arrived.

Valerie stepped out of her heels and sighed as she squished her feet into the carpet. "You were babbling earlier. Explain exactly what's going on."

"I need a drink first."

She gave me a simpering smile. "I'll make tea."

"A real drink."

"No, you have work to do, and you need to talk, or maybe confess is a better word?" She gave me a pointed look.

"I haven't killed him or even punched him. I've thought about it, but . . ."

"I'm sure you have." She studied me for a few moments. "But I think there's a little more to your relationship with Nate than you've told me."

"My 'relationship' with Nate consists of trying to thwart his attempts to waste Kingston's funds on projects that are essentially charity."

"Right." She might as well have said *bullshit*.

Did she know? I studied her. I was certain she did, but no way in hell was I making any kind of confession.

She bustled around the kitchen for a few moments, putting water on to boil, pulling tea, a teapot, and cups from a cabinet. How did she know where everything was when I couldn't find anything myself?

"What kind of tea do you want?" Valerie asked.

"What kinds do I have?"

She turned to look at me. "Are you kidding? You really don't know?"

"It's not like I shop for my own groceries."

"But I assumed you ordered what you liked."

I shrugged. "I don't think much about it."

She shook her head. "We'll go with Darjeeling. Have you ever even used these cups?"

"I don't normally sit around sipping tea."

"Busy with more nefarious pursuits?

"Here's a confession for you: half the time I sleep at the lab."

She studied me a few seconds. "That explains it."

"What?"

"That worn out look you have. People probably mistake it for grief."

Worn out? She better be joking. Just because I didn't sleep as much as "experts" thought I should—and had hardly slept at all since my father died and fucked me over—did not mean I'd let myself go.

"Can I just tell you what Nate has done?"

She laughed.

The sound warmed me. I was so lucky to have Valerie to listen to my rants. "Sometimes I think it would be a lot of fun to be married to you."

She set a tray down on the coffee table and joined me on the couch. "You think wrongly. I would've killed you within the first few weeks."

"Probably."

She handed me a cup. "Now talk."

I filled her in on Nate's proposal and how it was all a trick because he already had a plan written up.

"I don't think that qualifies as tricking you. Besides, his plan is unlikely to work since he didn't know the company was in trouble."

"But it's a start and now I have a tight deadline."

"If you knew how bad things were, why didn't you already have a plan?"

Why didn't I?

You were too busy being pissed at your father.

"Your point is?"

"You're pissed off that Nate's more prepared than you."

I tried to drink some tea but it was too hot. "Remember how I said I like that you don't sugarcoat anything?"

"Yes."

"I was lying."

"No you weren't. Now do your genius bit and come up with a plan."

"I'm fucking trying."

She delicately sipped her tea, not appearing the least bit ruffled. "Talk it through with me. That's what you called me for, after all."

At least she'd dropped the confession idea. I started describing some possibilities to her, going around in circles at first, throwing out anything I could think of, and then slowly, things began to fall into place. I ended by saying, "It's daring, but I think I can pull it off."

Valerie looked at me like I'd lost it. "It's insane."

"Insane may be what we need. My father was holding me back."

"Your father made some mistakes—" She held up a hand when I started to interrupt. "Plenty of mistakes, but he would've been right to question this plan."

"While spending all our money on safe companies that don't make us any profit."

"True, but—"

"I'm going with this. I'll just have to be at my most convincing, but I've seduced the board before."

Valerie raised her brows and gave me a you've-got-to-be-kidding-me look.

Was my plan too crazy? No. No more doubts.

"Let's go out and celebrate the win," I suggested. "I haven't taken you to my new favorite cocktail bar."

Valerie shook her head. "It's too late. You should be in bed. I think you may have gotten delirious."

I glanced at my phone. "Shit! It's 2 a.m."

Valerie nodded.

"You probably meant to go to bed long before now."

She stood and kissed my cheek. "I've never minded missing sleep for you."

"Thank you. Not just for this, but for . . . understanding."

"You mean well even when you're being an ass."

"What was all that about my 'relationship' with Nate?" Why was I probing that? The last thing I needed was Valerie on my case about wanting him, and yet I couldn't stop myself.

"It's late and that's a long conversation. Let's have it after you beat his ass at the board meeting." She slipped her shoes back on.

"Will I?" I asked as we walked to the door.

"Maybe or perhaps you'll actually learn how to compromise." I started to argue but she laid a finger over my lips. "Good night."

"Good night," I mumbled, closing the door behind her.

Chapter
FOUR

"$\mathcal{S}$o, if we're the first ones to get this to market then the proceeds will be enough to get us back on track."

There. My whole plan laid out. I exhaled and sank back into my chair.

No one said a word. Nate's mouth was hanging open. I guess I did get a little manic.

I glanced at the faces of the board members. Their expressions were just as stunned.

"Amazing, isn't it?" I asked.

"Is this a joke?" the board president Marsha asked. "We don't have time for jokes."

"What? No. If we want to bring in more money, the answer is innovation. If we use our Research division as we should—to develop new products for our businesses to produce—we can turn things around."

"A flying suit? We're not a comic book studio."

"It's not for a superhero. It's for recreational use, and—"

"You actually expect us to consider this outrageous suggestion?"

"Consider it. Approve it. Send me off to get working on it."

Marsha just glared at me.

"You're not entertaining *his* plan, are you?" I gestured toward Nate. He'd already given his proposal, which included a long list of cutbacks, changing timelines, selling off some of our recent acquisitions to cut overall expenditures. "It won't work. The severance packages he wants to offer would break us." I sneered at Nate. "Did you even take math in school? How could you—"

"Enough." Marsha's tone said not to push her further. "Nate's plan has a lot of good points, but it's financially unviable. We can't feasibly develop your . . . radically innovative ideas nor enact his warm and fuzzy ones. Cuts must be made, and we need to focus on obvious money makers."

"Yes, like my—"

She shook her head. "Look, both of you are incredibly talented though in different ways."

"Unlike Mr. Thomas, I can do math."

Nate glared at me and Marsha held up her hand. "Work together. Come up with a joint plan before we meet again in two weeks. Take it seriously this time."

"I'm very serious," Nate said. "I'm not laying people off and sending them—"

Martha shook her head. "This is the real world and we can neither fly nor can we make everyone comfortable and happy. Give me a plan that can work."

I grabbed my bag and left without saying another word, because everything I had to say was profane and a lot of it would permanently burn bridges.

Valerie was right. They thought I was crazy. "Goddamn it!" I slammed my fist against the wall as I stomped down the corridor.

Wow! That fucking hurt. At least the pain gave me something to think about other than the fucking idiots on the board.

I pushed open the door of my office and threw my bag onto a chair, not caring if my laptop survived the rough treatment. I had plenty of funds to replace it. If Kingston collapsed, I would hardly starve. I had money from my mother, money my father couldn't give to Nate. But no matter how well off I was financially, failure wasn't an option. If I lost Kingston, I'd no longer have a purpose, and the people I worked with, the researchers I'd brought in who shared my vision, they'd all lose their jobs.

Then make a realistic plan.

I wish to God I could.

I dropped my head into my hands and tried to block out everything.

Breathe. In. Out. In.

Fuck! I needed to get drunk, high, thoroughly fucked, to make it all go away.

That is not the answer.

It's the only one I've got.

"Mr. Kingston?"

It was my assistant, Brad. The worry on his face told me he wanted to help. He seemed sincere, but I didn't want to talk to anyone.

"I'm fine."

He raised his brows. "Can I get you anything?"

"No, leave me alone."

He glanced down at the tablet he was carrying. "Should I reschedule your next meeting?"

"Reschedule all my meetings today."

"Are you—"

"Just do it!"

He took a step back. "Yes, sir."

Fuck! I hadn't meant to take my anger out on him.

Brad returned to his desk outside my office and I slumped into my chair, dropping my head into my hands. What the hell was I going to do now?

I don't know how long I sat there with figures, innovations, and new product ideas whirling in my head, but eventually the door banged open. I jumped and looked up.

"Stop!" Brad yelled. "Mr. Kingston isn't available." He appeared in the doorway behind Nate.

Nate's hands were fisted like he was ready to punch something, maybe me. Was that what I needed? A fight? A long, punishing fight that maybe ended in . . . Hell no! No fucking the enemy.

Brad glared at Nate as though contemplating whether he should physically drag him from my office. I held up a hand. "It's okay, Brad. I'll deal with him."

"Yes, sir."

I gave Nate my best imperious look. "I'm not available now. If you'd like to make an appoint—"

"Stop the bullshit, and tell me what the fuck you were doing in that meeting."

Impressive. I wasn't sure I'd ever seen Nate that angry. "I was trying to save this company."

Nate shut the door, whether for privacy or to kill me wasn't clear.

He started to say something and then shook his head. "This really isn't going to work, is it?"

"What? Us working together? I said that from the beginning." Was he even listening to me?

"Then we should figure out the most humane way to dissolve Kingston."

"Fuck, no. You should resign."

Nate raised his brows. "You planning to buy me out?"

"Are you for sale?"

He glared at me, pure hatred in his eyes. "Fuck you."

That might be a good way to blow off steam. I came far too close to saying that out loud.

Nate suddenly sighed. "What are you going to do if I leave? Fire the board and bring it all burning down around you?"

I ran a hand through my hair. "I don't know." Even though my plan was too radical, I had no other idea how to fix this shit, but I hadn't meant to confess that to Nate.

"Yeah, well I don't know what to do either."

We stared at each other until I grew uncomfortable as my mind wandered to things way more pleasurable than arguing about Kingston. It didn't help that Nate looked like he wanted exactly the same things that were racing through my mind, which made no sense.

I tore my gaze away from Nate and looked down at the stack of papers on my desk. "I'll write up a compromise plan tonight and I'll send it to you. First thing tomorrow, we'll hash through it."

"A compromise? From you?"

Couldn't he just take the peace offering and go? "Do you have a better idea?"

"Yes, the plan I presented."

I shook my head. "We can't afford it."

"But you thought we could fund your absurd flying suit?"

That did it. "I'm so fucking tired of everyone thinking I'm some kind of freak because I have ideas no one understands. I'm tired of fucking pricks like you thinking I don't care about anything—"

"As far as I can tell, you don't."

"For years, I've busted my ass trying to keep this company innovative. I barely sleep, some days I forget to eat. I took the research department and made it count, and you know what else I care about?"

"What?" Nate asked.

"I care about getting you the fuck away from my company."

Nate's eyes narrowed and he took a step closer. He was angry, way fucking angry. And well built and— Oh shit. He looked ready to tear me apart.

"I. Am. Not. Walking. Away." He jabbed a finger at me to punctuate every word.

Whoa. As much as I wanted to focus on the problem at hand, angry Nate was fucking hot. And so close. I took a few steps backward. Since when was I the one who retreated?

I shoved him and he stumbled. "Are you going to fight me for Kingston? Is that your plan?"

He fisted the front of my shirt and drove me back until I hit the wall. "You think I can't take you down?"

"Finding out might be fun."

Something like lust flared in his eyes for a second. He let go of my shirt, but he leaned in, pinning me to the wall. Anger pulsed around us. Was he going to beat me or fuck me? Did I even care?

"Is that what you really want?" he asked. "A fight?"

I couldn't breathe. I was half hard. Part of me wanted to kiss him, but my brain told me to push him away and run. I shook my head.

He smiled but it didn't soften his expression at all. "I didn't think so."

I'm not sure which of us moved first, but suddenly we were kissing and God it was good. Nate's mouth was warm, his tongue slick as it slid along mine. He cupped my face to keep me where he wanted me, but getting away was the last thing on my mind, because apparently my desire for him wasn't as one-sided as I'd thought.

I grabbed his ass and pulled him closer. He fit perfectly in my hands, and his muscles were so fucking firm. How much time did he spend working out?

I should've broken away and told him to stop, told him I didn't want anything to do with him. But my cock was too fucking hard for me to deny what I was feeling, and I was too into the pleasure of the moment to voice any bullshit excuses. Nate seemed just as far gone. He rubbed against me and his firm body, all of that power, had me ready to beg.

Then Nate pushed at my shoulders and my head hit the wall. He stared at me, as he sucked in big, ragged breaths.

I couldn't get any air at all. Nate fucking Thomas had kissed me . . . or kissed me back. Either way I could hardly believe it.

His expression hardened. "You know my secret, and now I know yours. Don't fuck with me again."

He turned and walked out.

I brushed my thumb over my stinging lips as I stood there, watching him go. "So much for you being the nice one."

What the fuck did he mean? Had he kissed me just so he'd have something on me? Did he not want me after all? That was a fucking humiliating thought. Would he really out me if I didn't go along with his plan?

Fucking bastard!

I'd been sure Nate hated me so I shouldn't have been surprised by his threat. But his kiss told me he wanted me too, as badly as I wanted him. He hadn't been faking that.

As if things hadn't already been bad enough, knowing we wanted to fuck each other as much as we wanted to fight wasn't going to help us compromise.

And now I was supposed to write up some plan we could both agree to. If I'd known how to do that, I would've presented it to the board today.

Maybe we should spin off the Environmental division but include some other areas I didn't deal with directly. If we ended up with two more profitable, easier-to-manage, smaller companies, would Nate agree? This plan would lower overhead for Kingston, and I'd get Nate out of my hair. Financial recovery and independence: exactly what I wanted. So why not?

As my idea coalesced, I began frantically typing up notes. Moments turned into hours, and I stayed up most of the night working on my proposal.

He's never going to go for it.
It's not like he's got a better idea.

I considered calling Valerie, but she would just tell me this was another fake compromise. Was it though? Nate would get an awesome deal by having his own company, right?

Hopefully he would agree. One way or another, we'd see the next day.

Chapter
FIVE

I was sitting in my office late the next morning, staring at a model of the flight suit I wanted to work on, but not really seeing it. Columns of figures flashed through my mind, the ones that told me we were losing money so fast we wouldn't be able to keep afloat for long. I'd spent most of the morning on the phone, talking to various division presidents, none of whom had any good news for me.

More fuck ups. More delays. Should I fire everyone and start over? I sighed. What was I going to do? I was in way over my head. My dad had been right, and I hated admitting that, even to myself. I didn't have the business background I needed to run the company. I was a scientist and that's what I wanted to be.

You could actually listen to the board and do what they suggest.

But they never say things I like to hear.

You're so fucking spoiled.

I had nothing to say to my conscience about that. I was, and that wasn't likely to change.

My phone rang. It was Nate. I braced myself before answering.

"Adam Kingston."

"How the fuck is the Enviro division supposed to work without the resources from Corporate Research?"

"No greeting? Not a simple hello or good morning?"

"Answer my question," he demanded. "While our own researchers might take care of our short-term development, we rely on the Research division for our long-range innovation and the equipment that doesn't fit our budget."

"You'll find a solution or you'll hire the work out."

"With what capital?"

Why was he so fucking exasperating? "That will be for you to decide."

"This proposal is nothing but bullshit. Do you even know what a compromise is?"

"Compromise my ass. You do that shit to me and walk out, and you think I'm going to work hard to make you happy?"

"*Do* that? You mean kiss you? Don't act like that wasn't mutual."

I snorted. "I'm not the one who walked away."

"Fine, you won't talk to me. I'll just come up with a better plan."

I rolled my eyes. "As if you can."

"I'll have it to you by the end of the day."

Nate got a proposal to me as promised, one that I was never going to agree to. He hadn't reserved enough funds for innovations and had made only slight cuts in our unproductive areas. I spent all day and into the evening altering his plan. I accepted about twenty-five percent of it, barely able to stomach that, and then sent it back.

I expected to hear back from him quickly, probably a tirade about what an ass I was. I didn't care that it was now close to ten thirty. If I was working, Nate could be too. Patience has never been one of my virtues, and I'd waited long enough, so I called him. He didn't answer his phone. Was he blowing me off? Hell no, that was not going to happen.

I pressed the intercom button. "Brad, are you still working on those files for the Interweave account?"

"Yes, sir. Did you need something?"

"No, I'll handle it. You should head home." I should've sent him home hours ago. I took advantage of him far too often.

"Are you sure you're okay? You seem especially tense, even for you."

"I'm fine, or no worse than usual. Now go get some rest." I'd find Nate myself.

I called Michelle, his assistant. I was expecting her voice mail to pick up when she finally answered.

"Mr. Kingston, is something wrong?"

It was clear how much she disliked me from her tone. What had Nate told her about me, that I experimented on kittens and babies?

"I need to see Mr. Thomas immediately, and I'm hoping you know where he is."

"Sir, are you aware what time it is?"

"Time for me to find him."

After a moment of silence, she said, "He was still at the office when I left. That's all I know."

She knew where he was or could at least guess. I was sure of it.

"If you hear from him, tell him to call me."

"Yes, sir, I will, but I doubt he's going to contact me this late."

I hung up and called the front security desk. "Did you see Mr. Thomas leave the building tonight?"

"Not by this entrance, sir, but I've only been on duty since eight."

Despite Nate's status in the company, he often rode the train and then took a city bike to work. He could call a car to pick him up, but no, Mr. I-Refuse-To-Act-Privileged was determined to hold onto his "normal" life. Thus, the co-owner of one of the largest companies in the country rode a bike while wearing an off-the-rack suit. It was enough to make me shudder.

If he'd ridden to work today, he might have gone out the side door in the lobby. It was closer to the bike rack.

"Check the footage. See if he left by the Wells Street side door any time in the last hour."

"Is something wrong, sir?"

"No, I just need to confirm if he's here. Call me back when you've checked."

"Yes, sir."

It was good to be obeyed, even though I was fairly sure I'd lost my mind. A few moments later my phone rang and I answered. "This is Lawrence from security."

"I know who you are!"

"Yes, sir."

Shit! I hadn't meant to snap.

"He left about an hour ago, sir."

"Thank you."

Where would he have gone? If only Michelle would talk to me instead of being so overprotective of him.

Valerie wouldn't be any help either. She'd just scold me for stalking him, tell me to let him blow off steam until the morning. I wasn't going to do that. Nate and I were going to hash this out tonight.

After college, I'd rarely used my hacking skills except to spy on Kingston business my father tried to hide from me, but when I did, breaking the intricate code still gave me a buzz, almost as much of one as I'd gotten from Nate's kiss. Fuck. I needed to erase that memory.

It didn't me take long to track Nate down once I got access to his texts. He was at a gay club called Ass-some. I'd been there once or twice, though I'd never had Darryl drive me, but I had few secrets from him. He'd been my personal driver for years, and he'd proved himself loyal.

When Darryl pulled up in front of the club, I took a deep breath. This was probably a really stupid idea. Usually when I went out, I took more precautions to keep from being recognized. But tonight, all I could think about was finding Nate. If someone saw me, I'd try to bluff my way out. I doubted the pretense of being there on business would hold, but I would think of something. I wasn't turning back now.

"Are you sure you want to go inside alone, Mr. Kingston?"

"Thanks for the concern Darryl, but I'm fine."

He frowned. "You'd be better off with protection."

"Not this time."

"But sir, I don't think—"

"I don't need a babysitter. All I plan to do is collect Mr. Thomas. Wait here for us."

"Yes, sir." He gave me the impassive you're-crazy-but-I'm-paid-to-do-what-you-say-anyway face.

"I'll have security on call in case you need assistance."

I shook my head and walked away. As I reached the door, I could feel the music inside. The line of hot young men waiting to get in had me wishing I had time to actually enjoy myself tonight. I could find someone to help me work off some stress if I weren't so fucking pissed at Nate. Or if my fucking father hadn't put me in this situation to begin with.

My thoughts stopped when I stepped inside. Men moved on the dance floor, bodies sliding against each other. The air was hot, sticky, almost tangible. How could anyone help being turned on here? Men. Women. Whatever their preference, they had to react to the sex-charged air of the place. I wanted to find a willing man, drag him to a private spot, and fuck him mercilessly without worrying who saw me or what they thought.

I moved around the edge of the dance floor looking for Nate. When I didn't see him, I headed for the bar.

"What can I get for you?" the bartender asked. He was hot in that surfer way, and he smiled at me as if he wanted to do a lot more than make me a drink. Of course, he probably made his tips by doing that to all customers.

"Scotch on the rocks."

"That's quite the Daddy drink."

Was I that old? It felt like it sometimes.

I'd only taken one sip when I spotted Nate. He was wearing a black tank top, jeans that were impossibly tight, and holy-fuck-me-now pink lipstick. He bent forward as a man ground up on him from behind. The movement caused pink lace to peek above the waistband of his pants. I barely stifled a groan. His ass was fucking perfect and the thought of lace stretching over those firm cheeks had me instantly hard.

You should leave. This is a mistake.

But Nate turned and saw me before I could get the fuck out of there. He gave me a once-over and a slow smile. Those pink lips were so inviting, and the fucker knew what he was doing to me. But no matter how much I wanted him, I'd come here to confront him, not to fuck him, so that was what I was going to do.

He pulled the man he was dancing with against him and whispered in his ear. Then Nate let him go and stalked toward me. His wide shoulders and bulging biceps contrasted wildly with the lipstick and what I now knew for certain he wore underneath those jeans. Nate Thomas, aspiring CEO, in manties should be ridiculous; he was anything but.

Nate stepped close and glared at me. "What are you doing here?" he asked, a challenge in his voice.

"Coming after you."

Nate's eyes widened for a moment. Did he think . . .?

I cleared my throat. "We need to hash through this fucking proposal. You're leaving with me, and we're going to make a new plan—or rather you're going to approve the changes I made to your shitty one while you were out playing."

"Right, because you're a paragon of virtue who always does what's expected."

I swept my eyes up and down him, trying not to get distracted. "At least I look like someone who runs a company." That was a stupid comeback. We were at a club, not the office, but I wasn't about to apologize.

Nate laughed, but the sound was bitter, mocking. "At least I do what I want and have no problem admitting what I like."

"Oh I know what I like, but I have more sense than to pursue it."

"Do you?"

Did I?

"How did you find me here?"

Not a subject I wanted to deal with. "I have ways."

"What ways? The only people who know I'm here are a few friends. I don't think you know any of them."

I shrugged. "Maybe I do."

"No, not these friends. And I didn't text them from my corporate phone, so you couldn't have found out that way." He studied me, his face growing redder. "You didn't."

My face must have given me away.

"Oh my God, you son of a bitch. You hacked my phone."

"Shhh!"

He grabbed my upper arms and squeezed hard enough to leave bruises. "Don't you shush me. How dare you—"

I broke his hold and held up my hands in surrender. "I overstepped. It was a mistake. I won't—"

"I ought to fucking prosecute you."

"No, you ought—"

He leaned closer until he was right in my face. "You do that again and I will make sure the board knows about it and that you suffer. You do not invade my privacy. You—"

"I'm sorry, okay?" My tone was disgustingly conciliatory. "Can we just go?"

"Did you just apologize?"

I nodded. "Yes, I did." And Valerie said I didn't know how.

He opened his mouth like he was going to say more and then shook his head.

"Come on. Let's go." If we kept this up, people were going to notice and then we'd both regret it.

"I'm not going home with you, Adam."

I didn't have time for this. "Yes, you are." Nate turned to walk away but I grabbed his arm. "Kingston Corp. should be mine. I may not have a choice about sharing it with you, but I will not let you destroy it. We're going to finish this tonight."

His eyes hardened. "Are we really?"

"Yes." We were still talking about business, weren't we?

Nate ran his tongue over his pink lips. "We could settle things here."

My heart hammered as Nate looked down at me. I let my gaze wander over his bare arms. They were amazing enough in dress shirts, but like this . . . *And that fucking lipstick. Dear God.* The thought drew my attention back to his mouth. I wanted it on me right fucking then.

Pull yourself together.

"Approve my revision, and we can be done with this."

"I'm not signing anything that doesn't include better provisions for anyone who's laid off and more of a focus on quality control."

"I could tell the board about all this," I said, gesturing to his outfit and around at the club.

Nate froze. Horror flashed across his face before anger replaced it.

My throat constricted, and I forced myself to swallow. What had I done? No matter how angry I was, I'd never use his sexuality or his kinks against him.

I expected him to walk away. I would've let him go, but he yanked me toward the door. "You want to go to your place. Fine, that's what we'll do. But I won't roll over. I own half this company and I get a say, no matter what the hell I wear or who the hell I wear it for. And don't forget, I know your secrets too."

My conscience had been right. I'd made a big mistake coming after him.

Darryl's eyes widened when he saw Nate. So much for Mr. Impassive Driver.

"We're going to my apartment," I told him.

"Yes, sir," he said but didn't move.

"Now."

"Um . . . yes, sorry, sir."

Nate still hadn't let go of me. Damn, I hoped no one was watching us, hoping for a story or their ten seconds of internet fame. They could get quite a shot of the two of us like this. At least it would be free publicity for Kingston.

Nate didn't say a word on the ride. He hardly even looked at me. Most of the time he stared out the window and fiddled with a string on the hem of his jeans.

Darryl pulled the car into the garage where we could walk straight to the elevator and take it up to my penthouse apartment. That way few people would see us.

"Should I wait here, sir?" Darryl asked.

I glanced at Nate. "No, thank you," he said. "I'll get my own ride home."

"You can always call me or one of the other drivers, Mr. Thomas."

He smiled. "Thank you, Darryl."

My legs were shaky as we walked toward the elevator. I hated myself for it, but I was nervous as fuck about what would happen once we got upstairs. I sure as hell didn't think it was going to be us coming to an amiable compromise on the future of the company and singing "Kumbaya" together.

I unlocked my apartment, pushed the door open, and gestured for Nate to go inside.

When I'd closed the door behind me. I crossed the room and poured myself a drink. "Scotch?"

"No." His tone was cold.

"So what do you hippie types drink? Organic beer?"

"I like Manhattans, but I prefer a clear head around you." So he was going to try to take the high ground. Bastard.

"Are you truly clear-headed now? Didn't you have a drink at the club?"

"Nothing but water." He studied me for a moment. "Why am I here?"

"To settle on a joint plan once and for all."

He gave me a once-over. Scorn or interest? I had no fucking idea.

"Really?" he asked. "You had to come looking for me at the club? You couldn't wait until first thing tomorrow?"

"We only have until tomorrow night."

He wandered over to look out the floor-to-ceiling windows in my living room. "But if, as you said, I have no choice but to sign, I could easily do that in the morning."

"We both know that's wishful thinking on my part. I often state what I want as though it were already absolute truth. Most people just go along with me."

"I've noticed, but we could've handled it tomorrow either way."

I shook my head. "I'm not a patient man."

"So you came after me because you were impatient."

I nodded.

"Impatient for me to agree to your plan?" I had a feeling he knew exactly what I was impatient for.

"Why did you kiss me?" I regretted the question as soon as I'd asked.

He smirked as if I'd just confessed what he'd suspected all along. "Because as much as I find you arrogant, selfish, and possibly unstable, there's something about you that fucking turns me on."

Any chance of me not being hard for the rest of the conversation died then. "That's ridiculous. You can't stand me."

"True, and you don't like me either, but you sure as hell kissed me back."

"You're hot as fuck. I think you know that."

He gave a Cheshire cat smile. "How have you managed to hide the fact that you're gay all this time? I've never even heard rumors."

My heart rate sped up. I could hear it whooshing in my ears. "I'm not gay."

"Um . . . what just happened would say otherwise."

"I'm bisexual." There. I'd said it, even if my hands were shaking.

"So all those women weren't a cover."

"No."

"But all your men were dirty secrets."

My face felt like it was on fire. I looked away.

"What? No comeback?"

A wave of nausea and dizziness hit me. A full-blown panic attack was a possibility if I didn't get out of there. I ran to the bathroom and shut the door, barely resisting slamming it. Would he leave if I stayed there long enough?

Chapter SIX

A few seconds later, Nate knocked. "Adam, come out of there so we can talk."

I held on to the counter as the room whirled around me. "No."

"Come out, or I'm coming in."

"I . . ." My words died, because I had no idea what I wanted: his arms around me, or to disappear and never have to confront him.

Nate opened the door, and I just stood there, hands shaking, watching him in the mirror, wondering if I should kiss him or shove him away and lock him out.

"I want you too if that helps."

I didn't respond.

"Turn around and look at me, Adam."

I didn't mean to obey him. My body simply moved without my permission.

He took a few steps until he was right in front of me. "I'm calling a truce."

I had to swallow before I could speak. "For how long?"

"Until we finish with this." He gazed pointedly at my cock.

"So I'm just supposed to ignore the fact that Kingston is falling apart and I can't work with you?"

"That's right."

"How?"

He sank to his knees in front of me. "Because I'm going to suck your cock."

Fuck. "That's a good reason."

"Yes," he said as he unbuttoned my pants. "It is."

Nate opened my fly, but he didn't pull my cock out, instead he leaned in and nuzzled it. I tensed. He hadn't even touched bare skin yet and it was already clear I wouldn't be able to hold anything back from him.

"Relax," he said, his voice low and rough, his breath warm against me.

"I used to imagine you were Satan in hippie guise. Maybe I was right. You're absurdly good at this seduction thing."

He chuckled. "Stop thinking."

"I can't. That's one of the reason why I never—" He mouthed my cock though my briefs. "Holy fuck!"

"Like that, do you?" he looked up, his pink lips slightly parted, eyes dark.

"I . . . um . . . yes."

This time his smile was completely genuine. "Now I know what to do to make the sass stop."

"I . . ." Never finished. He shoved my pants and my briefs down and my cock sprang free and reached for his mouth.

"Mmm, you certainly do want this."

I groaned. "Shut up and get on with it."

"No talking. No moving either. Hold the counter and do nothing."

"You can't tell me—"

He raised a brow and my hands went to the edge of the counter. "Much better."

I didn't do obedient or submissive or . . . Nate. Yet here I was taking all his commands. He had me mesmerized as I watched his hand slide up and down my cock.

When he licked the tip, I jerked, unprepared for just how good that would feel. It had been a damn long while, at least based on my usual standards. I'd burned out on paying for sex—yeah, I did that and so do a lot of other people, don't judge—and gold diggers and hookups I regretted before I even got off. But Nate was different, not just because this wasn't sex-for-hire, but because he made me feel so much with just the touch of his hand. Being with him was already better than the last dozen rounds of sex I'd had and we'd hardly started.

He dipped his tongue into my slit, and I gripped the counter harder. No way in hell could I stay still and quiet for much longer.

After a minute, he finally took me into his mouth and I drew in my breath at the sight of those shimmery pink lips wrapped around my cock. If it weren't for my hands on the counter, my legs would have given way as he sucked.

He took me deeper and deeper still. Holy fucking God, Nate Thomas was deep-throating me. *If I'm dreaming, I sure as fuck better not wake up.*

He looked up at me and somehow managed to smirk with my dick down his throat. Talented asshole.

I scowled at him. "Get on with it."

He pulled off and I held back a whimper. "Keep up complaining and I'll stop completely."

"Please, don't."

His eyes went wide. That word "please" coming out of my mouth shocked him as much as it did me.

"You said forget how we really feel, right?" I asked, heat filling my face. Because the real-world Adam Kingston didn't beg, not even for what might be the best blowjob he'd ever had.

"Adam?"

"Yes?"

"Shut up and enjoy this."

I wasn't good at turning my mind off; I never had been. I analyzed, observed, and commented nonstop— *Fuck!* He swallowed me again, and the tip of my cock slid against the back of his throat. Dear Lord, could anything feel better?

Him bending you over the end of the bed, pounding into you, working you until you're dripping sweat, shouting his name, crying out for him.

My mind clearly hated me. I was going to come in seconds if I didn't stop thinking that way.

Nate sucked, kissed, and licked me until I needed to grip the counter just to stay upright. My breathing was ragged and when he took me all the way down, I made embarrassing whimpers no matter how hard I tried to hold them in. It was just so good.

He slid his lips along my shaft while he toyed with my balls. Then the bastard sank down until his fucking nose was against my pubic bone. I gasped. "Nate, Jesus!"

He stayed there for longer than should have been possible and then pulled all the way off, gasping for air.

"Fuck, that was . . ." I had no words to describe it. Nothing had ever felt that good before.

Nate licked his lips and nodded before starting to suck me again. His mouth was so fucking hot, and his soft lips sliding along my cock nearly did me in. My whole body tingled from the intensity. Why did we have to hate each other when he was so fucking perfect? I fought to suck in air as his slick tongue caressed the underside of my cock. I was close. So close.

He let me go and sat back.

"Don't stop." I no longer cared if I begged. I needed this, and I was going to have it. It wasn't like I could let it happen a second time. "I need more."

Nate rose to his feet. "Damn right you need more. Get on the bed."

Did he think I was going let him fuck me? Was I?

"I don't . . . I'm not . . ." I had no idea what I was saying. He'd completely rattled my brain.

He leaned in and kissed my neck. If I couldn't form a sentence before, I sure as hell wasn't going to be able to now. "I'm not going to hurt you," he whispered.

"But you will." We were enemies, at war over what we both thought of as ours to protect.

"Not like this, not here, not when I'm touching you."

That I could let myself believe, and while the aftermath might do me in, this was too good to give up. "Fine."

"So how do you want this to work? Do you expect to control everything in bed too?"

Why not be honest at this point? "I love to be fucked as long as it's the right person doing it."

He gave me an evil smile. "I *am* the right person."

His words sent a shiver through me. I had a feeling this was one time we were going to agree on something. "Are you?"

"Yes, and I want to bury my cock in you and hear you make those same sounds you did when my mouth was around your cock."

I almost made one then. "Do it."

"Only if you swear you won't try to use it against me later."

"I swear. I shouldn't have said what I did."

"Which of the many things?'

"About telling the board about you and your lipstick and . . . the rest of it." I would never have hurt him like that, but now that he'd shown how much he cared about my pleasure, rather than just getting himself off, I doubted I could even toss out spurious threats.

He took a few steps back, pulled his tank over his head, and tossed it on the floor. His hands went to the fastenings of his pants, and he undid them, slowly exposing a triangle of pink lace.

I licked my lips as he pushed his pants over his hips. Nothing could've made me look away.

When he kicked them off and stood there, in nothing but lace panties and lipstick, I knew I'd never seen anything sexier. Before I saw that damnable scrap of lace sticking out of his bag I would've said seeing a man dressed like that would do nothing for me. But Nate . . . The pink, combined with his toned body and a look that said he would fuck me until I screamed. It was too good.

We had plenty of time to hate each other after this night. So he was the last man I should have naked or nearly so in my bedroom. So fucking what?

"Get on the bed," he demanded again.

"Now who's bossy?"

"You like it."

I did. I didn't want to, but I did. I toed off my shoes, kicked out of my pants, and started unbuttoning my shirt. Nate batted my hands away. "I'll do it."

While he divested me of my shirt, I toyed with his panties, running my hands over the lace. The novelty of them on a hard male body was so fucking erotic. "I don't suppose you can fuck me with these on?"

He grinned. "Not these, but they do make ones with openings for that."

"I can see why." Too bad I wouldn't be seeing those.

"I didn't expect you to like them or to admit it if you did."

"I'm honest sometimes."

He nodded. "That's good to know."

I knelt in front of him and rubbed my face against the lace. Then I lowered them enough to run my tongue along the underside of Nate's cock. He dropped his head back and groaned as I licked the tip, while sliding my hand down the crack of his lace-covered ass.

"Can't last long if you keep that up," he gasped.

At least I wasn't the only one.

"Sucking you was incredible. It felt fucking fantastic to have your cock down my throat."

I sputtered around his cock. That he'd done that was amazing enough, but for him to say he loved it was too much. I pulled back. "Your mouth is amazing. I've never . . . You're . . ." Heat rushed up my neck. What the fuck was I doing? Exposing everything about myself to him, to Nate fucking Thomas.

"Get on the bed," he ordered. "I won't tell you again."

Thank God he understood that I couldn't talk about how I felt. Nate ordering me around I could deal with. Sex. Domination. A man riding my ass. That was territory where I was comfortable.

I slid his panties down his legs so he could kick them off. The feel of the lace under my fingers made me shiver with lust. I stood, hoping he wouldn't notice my hands shaking, then I climbed on the bed intending to get on my hands and knees, since clearly neither of us were in the mood to wait. But he tackled me, rolling me over and pinning my arms over my head. My breath caught as I looked up at him and felt something that went beyond lust, some deep need he touched.

Oh, fuck. Was it obvious I felt more than I would with a random hookup? Shit! What was I doing? I was naked and trapped under him. Panic rose and the edges of my vision grew dark. Breathe. Just breathe. Why did I pretend to be up for anything? I played like I barely had feelings, but that was all a fucking front. My feelings were as real as anyone else's, but I hid them, because exposing myself tripped an intense fight or flight response.

I was about to push Nate away, but then he leaned down and kissed me, and my tension melted away. His lips were warm, and they parted under mine. I slid my tongue into his mouth and tasted myself when I licked at the roof of his mouth.

"Keep your hands over your head." He let go of me and kissed my neck and then my collarbone. Then he flicked his tongue across one of my nipples, making me hiss.

He grinned up at me and did it again, then he nipped at the hard nub.

"Fuck!"

"Mmm." He sucked my nipple into his mouth, and I arched against him, but he grabbed my hips, forcing them down. I struggled but I couldn't get free, and I liked that. How did Nate know I needed him to take control?

He kept working his way down over my abdomen. He gave my cock a sweet, soft kiss and pushed my legs open, allowing him to kiss, suck, and bite my inner thighs. Soon I was squirming from the attention, ready to beg again. My cock needed friction, and even once he let go of my hips so he could move lower, all I could do was fuck the air.

"You're fucking torturing me."

He grinned. "Yeah, you're really suffering."

The way he was playing with me let me know this wasn't going to be a quick fuck like I'd expected. He was going to destroy me. He licked his way down my leg and then took my foot between his hands and massaged. I almost forgave him for leaving me hanging, because his hands felt incredible. His fingers dug into my arch, and then he sucked my big toe into his mouth. I would've said I wasn't into that either, but apparently with Nate I was into anything.

Nate watched me as he sucked the digit, and I bit my lip to keep from making those damn pathetic noises. I never expected him to take this kind of time with me, to build my anticipation, to make me feel so damn much.

"Stop holding back," he demanded. "I want to hear you."

"You're sucking my fucking toes," I said pointlessly as he started work on my other foot.

He glanced up and smiled wickedly.

"Fuck off." The asshole was laughing at me.

He licked my arch and I yelped. "That tickles!"

It also felt really damn good though. He stretched out over me, lined our cocks up, and thrust. The feel of his tight warm skin against mine was heaven.

"Good?"

"You know it is."

He was moving his hips so slowly, but it was better than when he'd been ignoring my cock completely.

"Lube? Condoms?" he asked.

I stared at him dumbly.

"I'm ready to open you up."

"Fuck." The word came out as a barely audible whisper.

He nodded.

I tilted my head toward the nightstand on the right side of the bed. "Bottom drawer."

"Don't move."

I didn't.

He came back with what he'd needed and coated his fingers liberally. "Turn over."

I wanted to watch as he pushed into me, but no way in hell could I fuck Nate Thomas face to face. This was much better. I could pretend it wasn't Nate. I could . . . Who was I kidding? I was more likely to pretend every partner I had from here on *was* Nate than to pretend I was with someone else now.

What the fuck was wrong with me? Could I make any worse choice in lovers?

I pushed my ass out further and rested my head on my hands. *Don't think about how exposed you are.*

Nate brushed a lubed finger over my hole, and I jerked away.

"Easy. I'll go slow."

I didn't want slow. Slow was part of the problem. Fast and rushed could be excused as temporary insanity, but this was a deliberate choice to let a man I hated bury himself in my ass. I started to roll to my side. "I don't know if—"

He laid a hand on my hip, gently pushing me back down. "Stay with me."

"O-okay."

My arms and legs were shaky and unsure as Nate teased me again, circling my rim while he worked my cock with his other hand. Soon I was thrusting into the hand and longing for more. But when he finally pushed inside, I tensed, clamping down on the finger, my body telling him to keep out.

Nate caressed my hip. "You can relax with me, I swear it's okay."

"I don't think I can."

"Do you want to fuck me instead?"

"I . . . I don't know."

"Turn over on your back."

That would be so much worse, seeing him, knowing he was seeing me. It would be so fucking hot and so very real. Too real. This was all getting too real. I rolled over anyway.

Then I gazed up at him, trying to figure out how to say he needed to leave without making everything worse, but the look on his face—concern, no mocking, no annoyance—made me reconsider. He was treating me like he did most other people. That was a Nate I never got.

Isn't that the Nate you dislike so much?

I thought so.

Nate straddled my thighs. "How about this? I ride you. That way your ass won't be sore but I can still hold you down and make you writhe."

"Oh my fucking God." How did he read me so well?

"Is that a yes?"

I nodded.

"Say it."

"Y-yes."

He grinned as he rolled a condom onto my cock. Just that touch was enough to have me working my hips, trying to get more. He slapped the side of my ass. "Patience."

"I told you I don't fucking have any."

"Then I'll have to teach you how to get some. God knows I've learned how to have endless patience working with you."

"I thought we—"

"Shh!" He lubed his fingers again and pushed two of them into himself.

I watched, mesmerized as he sank down on them. "Fuck, that's hot!"

"Yeah?"

I nodded vigorously. "I want to see more."

He worked his fingers in and out and then added a third.

When I'd waited as long as I could, I demanded. "Ride me. Right fucking now."

He shook his head. "I say when. Not you."

"The fuck you—"

"Go with it. You like it. And it's just for tonight."

I exhaled harshly. "Fine. Take your sweet time then, let me die of pent-up lust."

He laughed and rode his fingers faster.

"You've got to stop or I'm going to come from watching that."

He straddled me then, a satisfied grin on his face.

When he took my cock in his hand, I sucked in my breath. Then he started to lower himself, little by little. His thigh muscles were amazing, holding him suspended. I laid my hands on them, needing to feel them working.

"Truly fucking incredible." The words slipped out. But they made him smile, so I didn't care.

Finally, I was as deep inside him as I could go.

"Hands above your head," he ordered.

"Why?"

He raised his brows. "Because I'm telling you to, and I'm in control here."

"But—"

"No protests. Just fucking do it."

I did.

"Now relax and enjoy." He lifted himself and then slid back down, slowly, carefully.

I held my breath. He was going to kill me. Maybe that had been his plan from the beginning.

He groaned. "You're so fucking tense."

I tried to relax, but that didn't work, so I decided to see if I could rattle him. I wiggled my hips side to side, and then thrust up into him. He leaned over me, and I kept shifting until his cry of surprise let me know I'd found the perfect angle.

"Do that again," he demanded.

I couldn't have stopped myself if I wanted to.

I drove into him over and over, and he positioned himself to meet every stroke. We grew wilder, rougher. I wanted it to last forever.

Nate must have too, because he pinned my wrists down when I tried to stroke his cock. "No. I can't take that."

"I . . ."

"Yes?" he asked on a harsh breath.

"More!"

He began driving himself against me so hard we'd both be bruised. *I'd love that.*

Finally, Nate reached for his cock. I pushed his hand away to replace it with mine. I worked him with a tight grip that had him groaning. He had to be right on the edge.

Seconds later he cried out and come shot from his dick, slicking my hand as I kept pumping him. I was close too, my body so hot I thought it might catch fire. When his ass pulsed around my cock, I felt it all the way to my toes.

Nate thrust into the circle of my hand until he'd emptied himself completely. As the final shudders of his orgasm passed, he looked ready to collapse, so I rolled us.

As I let my weight rest on him, he groaned and the sound vibrated through me. Damn, he was hot. When he wrapped his legs around my waist, I held back for just a moment, savoring the sensation of his warm body. Then, I drove into him. His slick heat teased my cock. I squeezed my eyes shut. He was so fucking tight. I was so close, so—

I came and the pulses of my orgasm seemed to go on forever. Wave after wave hit me, and before I finished I made the mistake of gazing down at Nate. He looked relaxed, sated, and his expression was so open. He'd clearly loved this as much as I had.

"Fuck," I muttered as I pulled out.

He laughed. "Yeah, we did. Never thought that would actually happen."

I tossed the condom toward my trash can, then flopped on my back and covered my face with my arm. "Are we back to reality already?"

"Shit, I'm sorry."

"No, you're right this was—"

"Don't say it," he laid a finger on my lips. "Just let me get dressed and leave without hearing how much you wish you'd never met me, never wanted me, never—"

"That was the hottest sex I've ever had."

He gaped at me. "You . . . I . . ."

"That doesn't mean you shouldn't get dressed and go."

I couldn't read his expression. Relief? Disappointment? "We still have to—"

"We are not talking about Kingston while my bedroom smells like sex, and I'm waiting to see if bruises form on my hips from driving into you. Go home. I'll see you in the morning."

"Adam?"

"What?"

"I don't hate you."

I looked away. "You should."

Chapter
SEVEN

his time when I stomped into the bathroom, I shut the door firmly and locked it.

I immediately turned on the shower to block out the sounds of Nate moving around, but I didn't get in. Instead I sat there on the stool at the vanity, trying not to look in the mirror, certain I'd see something I didn't like. Vulnerability. Concern. Myself softening toward Nate. What if . . .

No, he wasn't right about Kingston. His ideas wouldn't work. But maybe . . .

Like he's going to compromise now after you fucked him and ran him off.

No! I couldn't let him leave. I jerked at the door, forgetting I'd locked it. "Shitfuck!" I turned the lock and opened it.

"Nate!" I yelled, but he was gone. I was too late to apologize, not that I knew how.

Call him.

My phone lay on the floor by my pants, taunting me.

The sooner you talk to him the better. It's only going to get harder.

Like this could get any worse. I was sitting here covered in Nate Thomas's spunk. I let him order me around, drag things from me that I don't give to anyone, and then I told him to fuck off.

Call him.

I was tempted to listen to the voice urging me on. *But he said the truce only lasted while we fucked.*

Maybe he just said that to get me to calm down and let go enough to enjoy what I was doing.

I remembered watching his face as I came buried inside him, hanging over him, surrounding him. That hadn't been a look of hate.

This was too painful. I should've just punched him when he'd kissed me. I might've broken my hand against his steely jaw, but at least I wouldn't feel so . . . bereft.

Somehow I forced myself to step into the shower and wash off all traces of Nate and what we'd done. If only it was as easy to wipe all memories of the day from my mind.

Once I'd cleaned up, I tried to go to sleep, but I lay in bed, tossing, turning, fighting the urge to jerk off to the memory of Nate sucking me, riding me, fucking unraveling everything I thought I knew.

After a few bouts of fitful sleep, sunlight was beginning to stream into the windows, and I was wide awake. Thoughts of how I'd screwed up with Nate swirled in my head. I needed to do something to hold them at bay. I stumbled into the kitchen, started a pot of coffee, and studied the goings on outside my window to distract myself until it was ready. A couple of cats were prowling the ledge of the building across from me. A flower seller was setting up a stall in the street below. The tree just below me seemed to be full of birds.

Beeeeep! The coffee pot pulled my attention back inside. I filled a mug, dumped a shot or two of whiskey into it, and took a few sips. Then I picked my phone. I had to talk to someone and there was only one person I could confess to.

"Hello?" a muffled sleepy voice answered.

"Valerie?"

"What time is it?"

I looked at the clock. It was only five thirty.

"Oh it's earlier than I thought. Sorry."

"Thoughtful as ever. What's wrong?"

"I slept with him."

"What? Who?" I could imagine her sitting up, eyes wide. I liked that I could still shock her occasionally.

"Nate."

"Wait. You slept with Nate Thomas? Your archenemy?"

"I did."

"I'll be right over. You'd better have plenty of coffee."

"I do. Mine's Irish."

"Maybe mine should be too, and order some breakfast. This is too much to take in on an empty stomach."

I said goodbye, dialed the concierge, and ordered two large hot breakfasts.

Valerie knocked on my door sooner than I expected. She must have dressed in seconds, but of course she was as impeccable as ever. I'd never been able to figure out her secret.

"Could you at least look like shit first thing in the morning?"

She laughed. "I'm a duchess, darling. That just wouldn't do." Then she whisked past me and poured herself a mug of coffee.

"Breakfast is on the way," I told her.

"Excellent, now tell me how the hell you went from contemplating Nate's murder to jumping in his bed."

"He was in my bed actually." I frowned at her. "Aren't you a bit surprised that I'm bi?" I'd called her because I needed her, but now that I was faced with the reality of telling her what happened with Nate, there was a knot in my stomach.

"I guessed that a while ago, and you basically confirmed it the other day when I said there was more to you and Nate than arguing over Kingston."

"You could act a little shocked."

"Adam, get on with the story."

I sighed. "Lust and anger are closely linked."

"In movies yes, but—"

"He confronted me in my office a few days ago."

"About your plan for Kingston?"

I nodded. "We argued. I shoved him. He shoved me back and then we were kissing."

She set her coffee down, closed her eyes, and exhaled. "Fuck."

"Yeah."

"Did you do that too?"

"Not right then. He told me off and left."

What if he was scared then just like I was last night? Maybe I wasn't so terrible.

No, I'm a right bastard. No way around it.

I sighed and took a sip of coffee. "So then he sent a proposal for fixing Kingston's financial issues. I made changes and sent it back."

She raised a brow. "You make that sound innocuous, but I can imagine the kind of changes you made."

"I made changes because he's not being realistic."

She snorted. "Neither are you. Adam, you don't know a thing about reality. You grew up being given everything you wanted and you think that's how the world works."

"Well . . . so did you." Wow. Great comeback.

"We're not talking about me. Let's focus on you and Nate."

I shook my head. "There is no me and Nate."

"Evidence speaks to the contrary."

I sat my coffee cup down so hard, liquid splashed over the side. "I made changes, legitimate changes, and sent them. He didn't respond, so I called. He didn't answer. I tracked him down."

"In his office?"

"No, at a club."

"Oh fuck."

"He was . . ." I paused. "This isn't something you can tell anyone."

"I think by now you know you can trust me with your secrets."

"But this isn't my secret, it's Nate's."

She nodded.

"He was wearing lipstick and panties."

"Oh. My. God." She fanned herself. "I wish I'd seen that."

I scowled at her.

"He's hot, Adam. You're not the only one who's noticed."

"No, I guess not."

"So you went home with him and fucked?"

"More or less."

She got up and poured herself a second cup of coffee. After she'd added cream and sugar, she asked, "How did you go from confronting him to jumping into bed exactly?"

"I told him he had to come home with me so we could hash this out for good. We were running out of time, because we meet with the board again tonight to report on our progress. When we got back to my place, he accused me of having ulterior motives for bringing him there."

"Did you?"

"I'm not sure."

She frowned.

"Not consciously, but I knew what might happen."

"And it did."

"Oh, yes."

She leaned in conspiratorially. "Good?"

"So fucking good."

"As good as you'd imagined?"

I tried to take a sip of coffee and realized my cup was empty. "How do you know I imagined it?"

"Anyone who likes men would imagine it with Nate."

The doorbell rang, saving me from her overly perceptive observations. "Our breakfast is here."

"Food won't save you from telling me everything."

"I'm a gentleman, I'm hardly going to—"

She laughed. "I didn't mean those details. Although . . ."

"Hush."

I answered the door, and gestured toward the coffee table. "Just leave the tray there please."

"Yes, sir."

"Thank you," I said as I handed the waiter a tip.

"My pleasure, sir."

I closed the door and was alone again with Valerie. She was going to drag the story out of me, but there were things I wasn't ready to tell myself.

She removed the lid from the tray and unwrapped the silverware. I sat as she handed me a napkin. What else was I going to do? Run away?

"So you knew?" I asked her.

"About Nate or about you liking men?"

"Yes."

"I suspected strongly."

"Why?"

"The way you talk about him like an ex-lover you hate but still want to fuck."

"I don't—"

Her expression told me to shut up. "And I've caught you noticing hot men the same way you do women."

That worried me a lot more. "Do other people know?" I picked up a piece of bacon and took a bite, bracing myself for her answer.

"I doubt it."

"Good."

She gave me a look that said she was disappointed in me.

"Look, it's not that I think being bi is wrong or anything, but I've got to think about my position with Kingston. There are plenty of people who wouldn't do business with me if they knew I liked men."

"And when have you ever cared what people think of you?"

"When it costs me money."

Valerie shook her head. "That's a shitty attitude even for you. What about when it costs you happiness?"

"I didn't call you here to have a coming-out conversation. Fucking men is just something I do. I don't need to talk about it, and there's no reason for anyone to know."

"Fine, but people will sure as hell realize you like men if they see you panting after Nate."

I scowled at her. "I have no intention of panting after him."

"Mm-hmm," she said as he buttered her toast.

"This was a one-time thing."

"You have those all the time—I assume sometimes with men?"

I nodded.

"So why is this one freaking you out?"

"Why is this . . .? Valerie, the man now owns half my company." *And he makes me feel too much.*

"And you hate him for that."

I shook my head. "I don't really hate him, but he infuriates me. He always has, because he's—"

"Gorgeous. Open. An honest man everyone likes."

"Fuck no, because . . . Sometimes I really hate how you call me on my bullshit."

She laughed. "I know, but I have no intention of stopping."

"I have to go to face him and finish our fucking plan which we never did because we were . . . fucking. What am I going to do?"

She finished a bite of toast before answering. "I take it things didn't go well afterwards."

"You could say that."

"What did you do to him?"

"Why do you assume it was me?"

She raised a brow.

I frowned. "It's not always me."

"No, it just usually is."

I drained my coffee and set the cup down. "Remind me why we're friends."

Valerie laid a hand over mine. "You need someone who doesn't let you play them, who isn't scared of you, and who isn't going to be a sexual conquest."

"Thank you." I squeezed her hand and sighed. "You know, my father was right about one thing; you're everything I should want in a woman. But I don't deserve you—or Nate." I set my fork down, no longer hungry.

"That's not true. You're an amazing man, or I would've stopped putting up with you years ago. You simply have a prickly exterior. Anyway, remember, I'm already married."

"He's never around."

She rolled her eyes. "Not when I'm in Chicago. He doesn't like to travel to America."

"Then why do you spend so much time here?"

"My life was here before I met my husband, and you know the saying 'absence makes the heart grow fonder'? It's true. I love him and we're happy, but we're both stubborn people and it's good to have time apart."

I poured more coffee for both of us. "I'm glad you're happy. If anyone deserves to be a duchess, it's you."

"Maybe Nate could do the same for you."

"Ha! We fucked. We're not—"

She gave me a pointed look. "There's more there. If there was nothing but lust involved, you would've resisted him instead of putting yourself in jeopardy."

"I hardly jeopardized—"

"He could out you. He's got a surefire way to manipulate you now."

I shook my head frantically. That was not going to happen. "I'm the manipulator, and remember, I know secrets about him too."

"Hmmm, then you two are quite a pair."

"No, we're not anything but business associates."

She smirked at me over the rim of her coffee cup. "Methinks the stubborn ass doth protest too much."

Don't let her see that she's right. "What? Why?"

"Your calculated surprise just now is a perfect example."

She took a last bite of eggs and let me stew. I'd still hardly touched my own breakfast, and her words weren't doing anything for my appetite, because it was true that if Nate didn't get under my skin in some way, if he didn't make me want like no one I could remember, things never would've gone so far.

"No matter what my feeling are for Nate. He's going to ruin this company if he's given free reign, and even if he agrees to my ideas, I wasn't supposed to have to share Kingston."

She sighed. "I know how angry you are. You think your father betrayed you."

I rubbed my forehead, trying to stave off a headache. "I was a shit son, and now I'm paying for it."

Valerie shook her head. "I wasn't saying that."

"But you're thinking it. Everyone is thinking it."

She set down her coffee and studied me. "Your relationship with your father was . . . Is it too cliché to say complicated?"

"Yes."

She smiled. "Well, complex then."

"He hated me. How complex is that?"

"No, I don't believe he did. I think he had trouble understanding you, and you didn't always make that easy."

That was an understatement. "I didn't want him telling me what to do."

"You had every right to find your own way but—"

"I should've tried harder. I know. It's too late now, and I'm stuck with fucking Nate Thomas."

She laughed, softly at first and then as I realized what I'd said and joined her, full on wild laughter.

"I didn't mean— Oh, hell." It took me several more moments to compose myself.

"There. Didn't that feel good?" she asked.

I slumped back against the sofa. "I guess."

"You really are going to have to talk to him if you're going to have a solution to show the board."

I shook my head. "I can't."

"You're a grown man. You can face last night's bad decisions."

Could I really? "How can I compromise with him after what happened?"

"So you're going to be childish. He can't fuck you and then get what he wants?"

"For the record, I fucked him."

"I thought you weren't going to share those details," she said as she stirred more cream into her coffee.

"I thought you wanted them anyway."

She flipped me off. Something about the gesture from a woman who looked as elegant as Grace Kelly was too much. My laughter threatened to turn into hysterics.

Valerie grasped my hands. "Adam, you have to try."

"Do I? I could just walk away."

She rolled her eyes and huffed. "What was your proposal that made him so angry?"

"That we split the company. He could take Enviro and a few other divisions."

"But not Research."

I shook my head. "No."

"Even I can see how that won't work."

"I knew it wouldn't work when I wrote it up, but I wanted to piss him off." I blew out a long breath. "I fucking hate this."

"Can you postpone the meeting, give yourself more time?"

"And admit I don't know what the fuck I'm doing? Hell no."

She took a sip of coffee, wiped her mouth, and then glanced at her phone. "I have to go now. Please do something. You can't talk to your father now but you can save his company."

"Maybe I'm just too damn stubborn."

"So you'll just go down with your ship when there are enough life boats for everyone."

"I'm not sure there are."

Valerie scoffed. "I am, at least if you're willing to get in one with Nate. Now walk me to the door."

I held out a hand to Valerie and pulled her to her feet. Then I drew her into a tight hug. "Thank you."

"You're welcome, as always."

We crossed the room and she kissed my cheek, before leaving. I closed the door behind her and then leaned against it. After last night, I not only wanted to save Kingston, I wanted to impress Nate with a solution, but would he ever compromise with me after the way I'd run off?

Chapter
EIGHT

*A*fter Valerie left, I sat there staring at the remains of my breakfast.

Get up, get dressed, and go make this compromise happen.

That's what I needed to do, but every time I thought about seeing Nate, panic shut me down. My heart raced, my head pounded, and I felt like I might be sick.

I didn't hate him. That wasn't the problem. But I was fucking jealous of him, and I liked him a lot more than I wanted to. I liked the way he looked at me, when he was trying to calm me down. I liked that when I relaxed enough, I felt taken care of when I was with him, something no one but Valerie had made me feel since my mom died.

I showered and dressed in my favorite suit. I might as well look and feel as good as I could if I was going to have to confront Nate. I glanced at my tray, but the food was cold and unappetizing. I didn't want to eat anyway. I was going to the office to read Nate's proposal again and take it more seriously. I was going to be an adult . . . in a little while.

I picked up the pile of mail I'd tossed on the counter yesterday. Going through it counted as important business. I flipped through the envelopes, tossing down a few bills and an ad for a cleaning service. Then I froze. A letter from . . . my father? What the hell? Was this a joke or had he found a way to plague me from the great beyond?

My heart pounded as I stared at the envelope. How could he . . .? He must have left it with his lawyers who were just now getting it to me. He always had liked those old-fashioned movie-type gestures. *Overly dramatic asshole.*

I took it to my desk and slit it open with the sterling silver letter opener that had always graced my mother's desk. I'd taken it after she died because I'd actually mourned her, actually wanted something to remember her by.

I pulled out the crisp linen paper, only the finest for a Kingston.

The letter was handwritten. He'd probably hoped the personal touch would sway me to whatever he was going to say.

Dear Adam,

I asked my attorneys to hold this letter until you'd had time to accept the joint ownership of Kingston.

I want you to know that I love you.

You had a hell of a way of showing it.

I've made a lot of mistakes.

Why yes, you have.

I'm leaving you poorly equipped to manage Kingston. I spent too much time ordering you around, because I was too stubborn to listen, which meant you never took the business courses you needed and I never got to mentor you in management.

I should have listened to your ideas even when I thought they were crazy. I should have valued what you had to bring to Kingston. You've done an incredible job of growing Research into one of our most important divisions.

Maybe you should've said these things to my face.

I gave up on us. I got tired of you telling me off, fighting everything I tried to do for you, and thinking you always knew best. I simply let you run with Research while I sought out the kind of business partnership I should've had with my son elsewhere.

I know you're angry that I haven't left Kingston solely to you. Angry and probably hurt, if you care enough about me to be hurt. But I did it for a good reason. You two complement each other. Even if you can't see it, I can.

Always right to the bitter end.

I wish things hadn't turned out this way. I wish I had more time to make up for what I've done wrong. I wish I believed you'd listen if I tried to. I spoiled you when I should've had you working beside me, even when your ideas were the complete opposite of mine, even when you told me off for being too old and dumb to know what I was doing. I made some choices that put Kingston in financial troubles, some of those choices are going to be hard for you to reverse in the coming months, but don't make the same mistake I made with you. Don't push Nate away like I did you. Listen to him. Say yes every time you possibly can. Bend. Consider. Accept that not everyone thinks like you. Basically, do everything I didn't do. You'll be so much happier than I was. It's too late for me now. I'm going to die bitter and sad. You still have a chance.

I don't have a chance with you, you fucking bastard.

I've missed out on years with you. Years I wish I could have back. I love you, I miss you, and I wish you the best with Kingston.

No. No. Don't do that. Don't you fucking do this to me. I crumpled the letter and threw it across the room as tears began to roll down my face.

"No!" I screamed. Tears stung my eyes but I fought to hold them back. I hadn't cried when he died, and I didn't want to cry now.

But I did, and not simply a few silent tears rolling down my cheeks. I sobbed, full body-shaking, moaning, snot dripping sobs. For a man who couldn't manage to say he loved me until after he was dead.

"Dead. Dead. Dead." I kicked the wall until my foot ached.

All those times during college and right after, when I'd just wanted him to listen to me for a little while, he'd been too busy. Not once had he said yes when I'd wanted us to do things together, and *now* he said he missed me.

"Fuck you, Dad!" I screamed so loud most of the other people in the building probably heard me.

I grabbed a bottle of Scotch. The glass I pulled from the cabinet slipped through my hand and shattered on the floor.

Leaving the Scotch on the counter, I stumbled into the bedroom. This was all too much. Maybe fighting was pointless. Maybe Nate should just have Kingston. My father never really trusted me with it anyway. I found my phone where I'd laid it before my shower, and typed out a text to Nate.

Do you want to buy me out?

I pressed Send.

A few seconds later, I sank to my knees by the bed. What the fuck had I done? I lay my head against the mattress, but that only made me feel worse. The bed smelled like Nate, like sex with Nate.

The room spun, and my vision darkened. *Oh, shit!* I tipped toward the floor.

Chapter
NINE

$\mathcal{M}$y phone rang for maybe the fifth time. Curiosity got the best of me and I looked at the screen to see who it was. Nate. I almost answered because I actually—despite all the reasons I shouldn't—wanted to talk to him, to let him comfort me. But that was stupid. Why would he want to talk me through a meltdown about the man who'd given him half of Kingston?

The phone stopped ringing and I checked the recent calls. Two were from Nate; the others were from Valerie. I powered the phone off and tossed it to the floor, not giving a fuck if it cracked. I was vaguely hungry, but I didn't feel like dragging myself from bed to see what I had in the kitchen. At some point, I'd pulled myself up off the floor and since then, I'd been lying in bed, drinking my way to oblivion. I poured myself another Scotch, wishing I didn't have such a high tolerance. I ought to be drunker by now. What time was it? The numbers on the clock were too fuzzy to make out. Still, what difference did it make? I closed my eyes and lay back on the pillows.

Pounding on my door woke me. Who the fuck was bothering me in the middle of the night? Was it the middle of the night? The blackout shades in my room made it hard to tell. I wasn't even sure what fucking day it was.

I stumbled into the living room.

More pounding. "Adam, if you're in there, you better open up right now." It was Valerie. "I'm giving you one minute and then I'm coming in."

Why had I given her a key? And what was she doing here now? I squinted so I could read the clock on the entertainment center.

Five o'clock. The sun shining in the windows suggested that was p.m., not a.m.

After banging my head on the door in a failed attempt, I looked through the peephole. Valerie was glaring at the door. "Adam, was that you?"

Oh fuck. Nate was with her, and he was saying something in a low voice. I pressed my ear to the crack of the door so I could discern their words.

"Have you heard from him at all today?" Valerie asked.

"Just one text." Nate's voice made my pulse speed up as I remembered his low dirty talk in bed.

"What did it say?"

Seconds passed without Nate answering.

Valerie sighed. "I know what brand of lube Adam prefers. I'm sure I'm allowed to read his texts."

Nate made a strangled sound and despite the sick feeling in my stomach, I laughed, quickly putting my hand over my mouth so they wouldn't hear me.

"You are not what I expected when I was told I was meeting royalty," Nate said.

"This isn't a Disney film."

Her comment set off another round of laughter, perhaps my despair was making me hysterical.

They were silent for a few seconds. Maybe Nate was re-reading my text. "He asked if I wanted to buy him out."

"What?"

I tensed, waiting to hear Nate's reaction.

"I assumed it was a joke. He knows I could never afford to do that."

"The fucking idiot."

Keys jingled, and my stomach flip-flopped. I really didn't want to see them, but Valerie hadn't been kidding. She'd let herself in before when I'd been here sulking. I opened the door and averted my eyes from Nate, sure I looked like shit that had been run over multiple times.

Valerie scowled at me and waved her hands, encouraging me to move back. "Let us in."

There was no point arguing with her. She wasn't going to back down.

Nate closed the door behind him. He wrinkled his nose as he gave me a once-over "Have you seriously just been drinking yourself into oblivion while we worried over you? You do realize the board meets in—" he glanced at his watch "—two hours and we aren't ready."

I wanted to scream at him, to tell him why I was such a mess, but instead I walked away without saying a word, not sure I could explain about the letter without having another meltdown. Nate and Valerie followed me into the living room, and I gestured for them to sit down. Both of them looked at me expectantly, so I pulled my father's letter from my pocket and offered it to them.

When Valerie took it, I retreated to my bedroom and shut the door, but I couldn't make myself cross the room. I wanted to hear their reactions.

"What is it?" I heard Nate ask.

"Oh my God. It's from his father."

I heard paper rustling.

"Wow," Valerie said after a few moments. They must have finished reading.

"Yeah." Nate's voice was almost too soft to hear. "I respected Adam's father, thought he was right about a lot of things, but this . . . this is cruel. He should've said those things while he was still alive."

"He was a fucking coward," Valerie said. "Maybe Adam was too at times, but he didn't deserve to find this out now."

"I'm going to cancel the board meeting. Adam's clearly in no shape to go. I'll tell them he's . . ."

"Got food poisoning?" Valerie suggested.

"Yes, that sounds good, and he looks as bad as if he did."

Thanks for pointing that out. But he was taking care of me again, when he could've simply screwed me over.

I heard rustling as though they were standing up. Then Valerie said, "I'm going to see if I can talk to him. Why don't you get us some dinner and bring it back? Then we'll see what happens."

"What should I get?"

Valerie took a few seconds to respond. "Pizza. Deep dish. I love indulging in American Italian when I'm over here, especially when I don't have to hear my husband rail about how wrong it is."

"What do you like on it?"

"I'm versatile, but for Adam. Meat. Lots of meat."

Nate snickered.

"Behave yourself."

"Yes, your grace."

I didn't like Nate sounding so easy with Valerie. She was my friend. Nate had half my company. I wasn't sharing Valerie.

I heard footsteps headed my way and I scooted back from the door, bracing myself for the scolding/pep talk Valerie intended to give me.

Could I talk about my father without breaking down? Would she push me to talk about Nate? I wasn't sure which would be worse.

Chapter TEN

Valerie opened the door just after I'd sat down on the bed.

"I'm sorry about the letter," she said, crossing the room to sit next to me.

If I started talking about my father I would cry or throw something, so I didn't respond. She sat on the edge of the bed and rubbed my back.

"Nate's gone?" Might as well keep up the pretense that I hadn't overheard.

"I sent him to get food."

I shook my head. "I can't eat."

"Well I can."

"I have a concierge desk." I gestured toward the courtesy phone in the entryway. "You could've called in an order."

She snorted. "I thought you'd like the idea of Nate being your errand boy."

"I don't like anything right now. Can't you just leave me alone?"

"No." Annoyingly she snuggled closer. "You clearly need help. Nate's going to call Marsha to cancel the board meeting. Were you intending to skip it?"

"Um . . . maybe. I sort of lost track of time."

"No kidding. When you didn't answer your phone all day, we had to come after you."

"I didn't want to talk to anyone after I . . . sent Nate a text, asking him if—"

"He would buy you out. He told me." Valerie squeezed my hand and I allowed myself to lean into her.

"How did he even meet you?"

She looked away. "Not important."

I chose to ignore that lie. "You know I can't deal with him now. Why didn't you send him home?"

"He's worried about you. He needs to do something for you himself. Unlike you, his first thought isn't 'Who can I get to do this for me?'"

"I can't help that," I huffed.

"I understand why, but that doesn't make you less spoiled."

"A fact my father was happy to pound home posthumously."

She put an arm around my shoulders. "Oh, Adam."

"Why the fuck didn't my father talk to me before? Why couldn't he—"

"Neither of you were any good at expressing your feelings."

"We lost all that time. And now I've lost . . . fuck, what am I going to do?" I dropped my head into my hands.

"You didn't really intend to sell out, did you?"

"At the time I did."

She rubbed my back. "And now?"

"I don't know. It's not like I have a better plan."

"You have to work with Nate to save Kingston."

I sighed and looked up at her. "How? I'm no good at compromising, no good at being diplomatic."

"True, but you have strengths and Nate has strengths, and you two are going to have to figure out how you can complement each other. Nate's willing to work with you, because he cares about Kingston too."

"Then why won't he—"

"Just do what you say?" Valerie arched her brow. "Because he knows neither of you have the right plan yet. You're neither one qualified for this."

"Yeah, that's way too clear."

Valerie glanced at her watch. "He's going to be back soon, with dinner. I'm going to take mine to go."

"Don't leave me with him."

"Adam, I can't solve this for you."

"I know but—"

Her pointed look told me she was done arguing.

"Fine. But don't be surprised if he comes back with kale, sprouts, and organic tofu?" I had to say something to lighten the mood or I was going to have to crack open another bottle of Scotch.

She rolled her eyes. "He's getting pizza."

"Deep dish?" I continued to pretend I hadn't listened in on every word.

"Just like you like it," Valerie assured me.

"How did you know that's what I'd want?"

"I have a lot of practice cheering you up."

She did, but I needed to keep things from getting too mushy. "I'm shocked that he eats meat."

"He does. Or he's making an exception for you. I would imagine he usually prefers his meat from ethical farms."

"I guess that's not too awful." I conceded.

"No, it isn't. In Italy—"

I waved her off. "I don't need to hear about the wonders of European food. It will just make me want to get on a plane."

"Then maybe you should consider that if the food industry adopted some of Nate's 'enviro-nut' beliefs, American food would be more like what you get in Nazapoli or most of the rest of Europe."

"Don't start."

A knock on the door kept me from having to hear any more about Nate's marvelous ideas.

Valerie let Nate in while I changed out of the wrinkled suit I'd lain around in all day. Then she found plates, napkins, forks, and a plastic container, which she filled with pizza. "I'm having mine to go."

Nate frowned, tapping his foot on the floor. What was he waiting for me to do?

Valerie kissed my cheek and headed for the door. "Play nice," she said. I flipped her off and she just laughed. "See? You're feeling better and you haven't even eaten the pizza yet."

"Even at my worst I'm ready to tell you off."

"That's my Adam."

She closed the door behind her, and the room went eerily silent.

Nate peeled off his suit jacket and hung it over the back of one of the dining room chairs.

"What are you doing?"

"I'm feeling a bit overdressed." He gestured toward me.

I'd pulled on sweats and a T-shirt, not wanting to bother with anything else. "If you think you can seduce me into agreeing with you, you're wrong."

Nate looked disgusted. "Adam, I'm trying to get more comfortable, not stripping for you. I get it, okay? You're hurt and angry and we're out of time. Let's just get this done."

"Okay." I made conscious effort to lower my voice. Between my father's letter, the need to focus on business, and the fact that I cared a lot more about Nate than I wanted to admit, my emotions were all over the place. Volatile. Wasn't that one of Nate's favorite insults during contentious meetings? But I had to meet him partway on this, and if I couldn't be honest, we weren't going to get anywhere. "I've been blaming you for things my father did, but that's unfair. It's true that I don't agree with all your methods or your vision for the company, but I don't really hate you."

Nate gave a half smile. "Like I said the other night, I don't hate you either."

Nate's approval mattered to me, more than I'd realized. My desire for him was . . . not as uncomplicated as I'd like. "You're good with people, with making them feel confidence in us. And I'm better with figures and innovation." I held up my hand as he started to protest. "I'm being realistic. Yes, I've focused on products that are long shots, but I believe they are worth the time. I also want Kingston to make money, preferably a lot of it."

"I'm not an idiot. My head's not so far in the clouds that I think we can stay afloat and not make a profit. We can't change the world if we go bankrupt, but I don't want to step on people in that process."

I ran a hand over my hair. "I know you think I'm a bastard for putting profit first."

Nate shook his head. "You're nowhere near as unfeeling as your father thought. He didn't know you any better than you knew him."

"But you do?"

"I . . . Well, a little."

I wanted him to know me better, but that was dangerous territory filled with inconvenient feelings. "Okay. Back to Kingston. Our marketing sucks."

Nate nodded. "I agree."

"Huh, there's one thing we don't have to argue about."

"I also believe Kingston is worth saving."

"That's two."

He unbuttoned his sleeves and rolled them back. I couldn't stop myself from watching. Did he have to be so fucking gorgeous? I wanted him again, badly, but a third thing we agreed on was that we shouldn't fuck again, so I wasn't going to bring that up.

He glanced up. Our eyes met. And he held my gaze, watching me like he was trying to read my deepest thoughts.

I looked away and cleared my throat. "Um . . . maybe we can find more we agree on."

"Yes, I believe we can."

Like how we actually did want to fuck again. And again after that. I couldn't help but wonder what he had on under his suit. Panties? Would they be pink like before or red or . . . Was there any color he'd look bad in?

What was wrong with me? My father had sent me a load of passive-aggressive guilt from beyond the grave, Kingston Corp. was in sad shape, and all I could think about was what was covering Nate's ass. Maybe I really was as useless as my father had assumed.

Nate and I spent most of the next day working through the plan he'd written and I'd edited. By late afternoon, I was exhausted, frustrated, and I'd done all the compromising I could stand for one day, for one lifetime maybe.

I threw my pen onto my desk and focused on Nate. "How do you do it? How do you sit there and act so calm?"

He shrugged. "I'm not calm. Inside I'm fucking terrified. But I'm not wound as tight as you."

I nodded. "I've always been like this, even before I knew the extent of Kingston's problems. I just need to be in control."

"I've noticed." Nate studied me for a few moments, but instead of more sarcasm, he pointed at one of the many pages of our plan.

"What if we consolidated this team from Household Products into Research? Couldn't Corporate Research do all their testing and innovation?"

"Probably, considering the current size of the business." They'd scaled down to less than half the size they were when Kingston took off in the 1970s. "But it will mean laying people off."

Nate nodded. "There are some low performers there."

"And you'll agree to offering them a package?"

"I don't like it, but it needs to be done. I know we can't keep everyone, not if we want to keep paying decent salaries. Speaking of which, we could lower our own pay."

I nodded. "Yes, we should." I could see the surprise on his face when I agreed without an argument. "It'll be good for morale to see that, and it's not like I need anywhere near as much as I make now, but what about you?"

"No one needs what I'm making."

"What if . . ." I could hardly bring myself to say it. "Things don't work out with Kingston?" A knot formed in my stomach and my chest tightened. I was surprised I'd even gotten the words out.

"I have a lot saved. Really, it's absurd how much I make. I have no clue how to spend it all."

"If you need help, I can give you some suggestions."

He laughed. "I'm sure you can."

We worked our way down the list of potential layoffs and spending cuts, actually agreeing on over half of them. We made a list of ones to argue over later.

"I think that's enough for today," Nate said, and glancing at my phone, I realized it was past what most people considered the end of the work day.

I sighed. "All we've done is find ways to cut our spending. We've not made a plan to generate more revenue and that's vital. It's the whole piece my dad didn't see. You can't just spend less. Sometimes you even have to invest heavily to make products that will be big earners."

"Just not so much you go under or on things that are pie in the sky."

I snorted. "Not all my ideas are crazy."

Nate smiled. "No, but we can't plan our product model around the ones that are an enormous stretch."

"Then what do we do?"

"Go home, get some sleep, and come back tomorrow."

"I hate how fucking reasonable you are."

He narrowed his eyes, studying me, and I liked the attention. "I think what you hate is having to admit that you're not reasonable."

I shook my head. "I've never claimed to be reasonable. I expect things done my way."

"And your way is best?"

"Usually, but you've made me concede a few points."

Nate grinned. "Maybe I'll get you to concede more tomorrow."

You could get me to concede my ass if you really tried. I wanted to kiss him, to strip him, to get on my knees and suck him off right there in my office but . . . What was even worse was that I wanted to please him, to make him like me rather than just not hate me. And that meant I shouldn't sleep with him again. Mixing work and fucking was bad enough, adding emotion to that was absolutely a no go. I needed to stay focused on the business. I was just going to have to forget the way looking at him made my heart race.

I shoved things into my briefcase, needing to put some distance between us so I wouldn't do anything foolish like asking him out, even if it was just to dinner and not necessarily for sex. Shit. I was in deep trouble.

"Adam."

I glanced up. "What?"

"Turn around."

"What? Why?"

"Please."

I couldn't refuse him, not with that earnest look on his face.

Nate settled his hands on my shoulders and I tensed, trying to find the strength to say no.

"Easy. I get that you don't want a repeat of the other day. But you're so goddamn tense, the way you hold yourself, your neck and shoulders must ache. Let me help."

I sucked at accepting help from anyone, and Nate . . .

He pressed his thumbs in at the base of my neck and I lost my train of thought. I almost lost my ability to stand. He began to work my knotted muscles and I groaned. "Fuck, that feels good."

"Mm-hmm."

His long-fingered hands moved expertly, his touch firm, reassuring, delicious though not overtly sexual.

"Jesus, Adam, how long has it been since you had a massage?"

"Forever."

"Yeah, it feels like it."

"No, really, I've never had a massage—not a professional one anyway."

"Why the fuck not? It's not like you can't afford them."

"I don't like strangers touching me." I stepped forward, out of his reach. His touch was making me want a lot more, but I'd sworn I wouldn't go there again.

"You want me to stop?" he asked. His words were soft and serious when he could have mocked me.

"No, I'm fine." I looked away out the window.

"I'm still just offering to loosen you up. I get that you don't want anything else."

I snorted. "No, you don't get it. I want everything else."

I heard his sharp intake of breath. Had he thought I was telling the fucking truth, that after the best fuck of my life I could simply stop wanting him? Surely he'd learned what a good bullshitter I was by now.

I took a deep breath and faced him. "I want you as badly as I did the other night." Worse, if I were honest.

He watched me, his chest rising and falling rapidly. I refused to allow myself to look down, because I didn't need to know if he was as hard as I was.

One of us needed to speak. I didn't want him to misunderstand, to think that anything was actually going to happen, because that would be disastrous, since Nate's gentle concern made me feel a whole lot more than lust. "The fact that I want you so much, that's why I can't have you touching me."

"You can't have a little and not want it all?"

"No, I'm far too spoiled." I looked away as if something out the window needed my attention. I couldn't bear the sight of his beautiful face anymore. It was taking all my willpower to deny myself what I wanted, and I'd never been accused of having much to begin with.

When he didn't speak for several moments, I did. "You can't honestly think that me— You— Us— That continuing what we started would be a good idea."

"*Good* idea? Maybe not. But I want you anyway."

"I thought you always did the right thing."

"Just because I don't like to fuck over my employees doesn't mean I'm some goody-goody. You saw me at the club the other night, didn't you?"

I nodded. Had I ever. Once I'd seen him on the dance floor, grinding up against another man, I hadn't been able to look anywhere else.

"So stop assuming you know so much about me," Nate said.

"And what, spend time quizzing you on your life history?"

"Maybe. It sure as hell would be better than the shit way you usually treat me."

"I've been doing my fucking best today."

Nate held up both hands. "Today is an exception."

He gently laid his hands back on my shoulders. I could have pulled away but I didn't, because as soon as he touched me, all I could think about was my first glimpse of lace peeking over his too-tight jeans. And his plump pink lips around my cock.

He squeezed hard, digging deep into my stiff muscles. It hurt, but in a good way.

"If you don't want me to do this for you, then go to a professional. It's not good for you to stay this tense."

"It's not too late for you to decide to sell me your shares. Then I wouldn't have to be so tense."

"You're bullshitting me again."

"Look at you learning how to read me."

He ignored my sass. "Would you really be better off on your own, shouldering all of this?"

"Yes." He dug his fingers in hard, making me groan. "No."

"Then we're just going to have to work together."

How was I supposed to work with him when every time I looked at him I wanted to get on my knees, unzip his pants, and find out what he was wearing under them? And—I swallowed hard—have him hold me afterward.

I shook him off. "I'm going home to rest up for another session of compromise-a-rama tomorrow."

"In other words you're going home to get drunk and try to forget that any of this—your father, the financial crisis, me—ever happened."

"Right."

He picked up his executive backpack and his helmet. Bike-riding do-gooder. "Have a good night."

"I think you know that's unlikely."

"Call Valerie if you need someone. I know you won't call me."

If I did, I'd have him naked in my bed as fast as I could. "Okay. Fine. Just go."

With a sad smile, he did.

I had to stop myself from calling him back. Even though I wanted him so bad it hurt.

Chapter
ELEVEN

That evening, I lay on my couch staring at the ceiling, contemplating the things Nate did well and how to use them. Business things, *not* sexual things. Well, I contemplated those too, but they weren't helping me solve any problems. I had a movie on, but it had become background noise.

As I reached for the remote to turn it off, my phone buzzed, so I grabbed it first. It was Nate. I debated not answering for a second, but decided to be mature. "What's up?"

"I've got a fantastic idea. I think I know how to fix some of our biggest problems."

"By giving everyone raises and spending a few years making all our products fit strict ethical guidelines?" I used a lighter, more teasing tone than I would have a few weeks ago.

"Right. That's it. How'd you guess?"

"Easy. Didn't you know I can read minds along with my other powers?"

"Damn, they forgot to tell us that in the how-to-deal-with-Adam-Kingston briefing at orientation."

"That's a shame. I'll have to see that they add it to the curriculum."

"I said we should regroup tomorrow, but I wanted to tell you about this now. We could get dinner if you haven't eaten."

"Dinner? Like a date?"

"Like a business meeting."

Of course that's all he meant. *What's wrong with me*? "Where do you want to meet? The Kale Cafe?"

"Ha! Do you like Indian food?"

"I love it."

"An honest answer with no snark. Are you really Adam Kingston?"

"Fuck off."

"There's an Indian place I love on Clark Street."

"Indian sounds good. I could have my driver pick you up, but I suppose you'll bike there."

"Actually, I'll probably walk. It's a lovely night. You could too, you know."

I sighed. "Fine. Just for you. I'll go on foot. See, I can compromise."

"Ha!"

He gave me the name and address and I hung up.

By the time I'd walked to the restaurant, I was starving. Nate arrived a few minutes after me. Fortunately, the waiter brought us naan as soon as we were seated. I had to force myself not to shove a whole piece in my mouth.

"You want to order several things and share?" Nate asked.

The dinner was feeling more and more like a date, but strangely that didn't bother me at all. "Possibly. What do you like?"

"I always mean to be more adventurous, but I love the traditional favorites like saag paneer and chicken tikka."

I smiled. "How hot can you take it?"

"As hot as you can."

I raised my brows. "I'm not so sure."

He looked me up and down and my cock stirred.

"Okay, this has to stop or I won't make it through dinner." I glanced over the menu. "How about we get your favorites plus lamb vindaloo, chili chicken, and raita?"

"Sounds great, but we're going to be stuffed," Nate said.

"You'll be walking home so it can all settle."

"Deal. I guess I'll have to hit the gym extra early tomorrow."

"I usually run at five thirty. You could join me."

He looked as surprised as I was that I'd offered. "Hoping you can leave me in the dust and mock me the rest of the day?"

"Well, that would be quite satisfying."

We placed our order. Once we'd gotten the bottle of wine I requested, I tried to turn my mind to business not pleasure. Since when did simply watching a man or bantering with him make me half hard?

Since you let yourself see the real Nate.

I took a sip of wine and then said, "So this master plan?"

Nate smiled. He looked so young and so fucking enthusiastic. I hoped this plan was as good as he thought, because I wasn't going to want to say no to him, which was unsettling as fuck since I loved saying no to people. The strength of his hold over me was unnerving. I'd never felt like this about anyone, man or woman.

"I think we should sell some of the smaller companies we've recently acquired."

Was that all? "I already said—"

Nate held up his hand to stop me. "That's a first step. I think we should also sell off Household Products."

Had he actually said that? "No." I might hate my father, but we'd both gotten our starts in Household. We'd had lean years but the division had potential to be profitable again.

"Let me finish. I know it was the core of the original business, the division your dad created, and it does make a profit sometimes. Barely. But it's not growing. It hasn't grown in years. If we divested ourselves of it—"

"No, Kingston is known for the Household division. Without that—"

"Now who's being sentimental when he needs to focus on profit? Research and Environmental are where we have the most knowledge, but they're also two of our strongest areas with the best potential for growth. Without Household Products sucking down so much capital, we can focus our energy where it will do the most good. We can also fund smaller projects in our next most profitable areas like entertainment. If we sell off Household Products, I think we can get back on track."

I had to force myself to close my mouth. If my father had heard Nate's suggestion, he might've died simply from that. Sell off the core of the business? Doing that seemed like giving up.

Sure, from a purely financial standpoint Nate's idea made perfect sense, I had to admit that—to myself at least. But I couldn't do it.

I shook my head. "No, absolutely not. We need to figure out another way."

"Why? What's wrong with the plan?"

"We're not selling Household Products."

"Because . . .?"

"Because we're not. It was where Kingston started and it's non-negotiable."

"So in other words, Adam Kingston is too stubborn to admit when he hears a good idea that's not his own." Nate pushed back from the table, anger darkening his eyes.

I laid a hand on his arm. "Don't go."

"What's the point of being here if you won't even consider the plan?"

"I'll consider it." Or at least pretend to, since I wanted him there.

"If we aren't going to talk business then—"

"Then we can simply have dinner?" If he left, I'd have to go back to my apartment and spend the evening utterly alone. That didn't sound as appealing as it used to.

Nate started to say something else, but stopped when the waiter appeared with our food. Once everything was on the table, Nate refilled our wine glasses. "A toast?" he asked when the waiter had walked away.

That was not what I'd been expecting, but I dutifully held up my glass.

"To finding a solution," Nate said.

I clinked my glass with his.

Our gazes locked as we each took a sip. There was no mistaking the heat that passed between us. No matter how anxious it made me, I wasn't going to deny myself the feel of his arms around me again.

We got through dinner without me dragging him out of there. We talked, but not about Kingston or anything else important. I think getting along felt too new to both of us.

"Would you care for dessert?" The waiter asked.

I shook my head.

"No, thank you," Nate said.

"Shall I bring the check?"

Nate nodded. "Yes, please."

He was so fucking polite and it seemed completely natural. He really was a better person than me. It fucking sucked to admit that.

You could always learn from him.

No, I'm too set in my ways.

"Are you too full for dessert?" Nate asked as we left.

"You can't still be hungry. You're the one who said I was ordering too much food."

"No, but I thought we could walk a bit and then get some ice cream."

Was it possible Nate didn't want the evening to end any more than I did? If he wanted me in bed again, he didn't need to seduce me with ice cream and walks. Sucking my cock had worked well before, although I would love to watch him lick a cone of ice cream.

"How about a drink instead?" I asked.

Nate was silent for a moment as if considering. Then he nodded. "Okay."

"I know a great place just down the block."

We stepped through the door a few moments later. The bar was modeled after an old-fashioned gentleman's club: dark wood, dim lighting, club chairs, gold floor lamps next to them, waiters in tuxes.

"Mmmm. Very masculine décor. Trying to take me some place where I won't order a girly cocktail?" Nate asked.

I sniffed. "Not at all." A week ago I would've challenged Nate to shots of whiskey, so we could see who could hold out the longest. But now . . . "I don't give a fuck what you order. They'll make you anything you want and even put an umbrella in it if I tell them to."

Nate smiled. "I'll keep that in mind."

A waiter approached us, one who knew me and my generous wallet. I might be a bastard but I tipped well when I got good service.

"What can I get for you, gentlemen?"

"I'll have a Manhattan," Nate said. Apparently he was only outrageous when it came to lingerie and what he could do with his hips.

"A Scotch for you, sir?"

I nodded. Then as he turned to go, I added, "Yes, please."

The waiter's smile gave away his interest. He was cute. I might've followed up on what that smile said if Nate hadn't been sitting there making me hard just from the way he was watching me.

Our drinks arrived a few moments later. Nate took a sip and smiled at me. "This is so your kind of bar."

"Yeah, it is."

"It's completely different from how it first appears, just like you."

I frowned. "What do you mean?" I thought I knew, but I wanted to make him put it into words.

"The bar appears to be for rich men, a place you go to pretend you can still live like it's the nineteenth century. Then you look around and see women, both straight and lesbian, gay men, young, old, different races. And it feels welcoming."

"I wasn't going to take you to a place where you'd feel uncomfortable."

Nate nodded. "I've learned that recently. A few weeks ago you—"

I laid my hand on his arm. "No. I might say shitty things, but I would never have taken you somewhere you'd feel ridiculed. Not even at my worst." I loved the way he studied me as I spoke, seeming to listen intently to everything I said.

"You're such a contradiction. You seem hard and selfish, but you do care. You just show it in different ways than I do, because you don't like for anyone to know how you feel."

"No, I don't." I'd pretended Nate didn't understand me earlier that day, but the truth was, no one besides Valerie had ever been able to read me like Nate. Of course, he'd seen me in the midst of a breakdown, and when we fucked, I'd let my mask come off entirely.

Nate glanced down at my hand, which I'd never moved. I slid my finger along his arm. His eyes widened and I smiled.

"Maybe we should go," I said, anticipation making me antsy. Would he take that to mean the night was over, or that we should go fuck?

"Let's go to my place. It's closer."

Sleeping with him was stupid and risky. Too much was at stake with Kingston for me to fuck up our relationship even more, but it was what we both wanted, and if there was ever a time in my life when I ought to forgive a few bad decisions, this was it.

I signaled the waiter.

"Shall I put this on your tab, sir?" he asked when he reached the table.

"Yes, please."

"Have a great evening."

"We will," Nate said and the waiter grinned.

Nate led the way as we exited. I moved beside him once we were on the sidewalk, wishing I could touch him immediately instead of waiting until we were in private. "You don't live in a hovel out of righteous indignation for people who have less than you, do you?"

Nate laughed. "No. I don't have a penthouse but it's a very nice apartment, and it's only a few blocks away."

"You could easily become a regular at Imperial." I wished he would.

"Are you there often?"

"Often enough."

He grinned. "Then I just might."

Oh fuck. My chest tightened and I felt cold and hot at the same time. My fight or flight reflex was in constant use these days, and it was hard to hide how bad my anxiety had gotten. I considered chickening out, saying I had to go home, but I wanted what he could give me. I couldn't pretend it was just fucking. That was what I'd done with other people. With Nate it was soul-wrenching and soothing at the same time.

Nate punched in the code to open the door to his building. It was a nice one, not as nice as mine of course but it felt friendlier.

We shared the elevator with an elderly couple. I wondered if Nate was as eager for us to get our hands on each other as I was. When the couple exited, I consider hitting stop and begging him to fuck me right there, but I managed to exercise patience.

When we reached his floor, he glanced back at me before stepping through the doors. Yes, he was just as worked up as I was. I could tell by the hunger in his gaze.

He opened his door and gestured for me to step inside. I wasn't sure what I'd imagined his home would be like. I hadn't really thought he'd have some hippie pad straight out of a 1960s movie, but I hadn't expected the beautiful yet cozy space I'd stepped into either. The apartment had a sunken living area that called to a person to curl up and watch a movie. Nate had decorated with bold colors and while things were clean, they weren't perfectly neat. His home looked lived in. Was that why it felt so satisfying, so unlike my place, which might as well be a hotel room? I was certain he, not a decorator, had chosen the art on his walls. Probably local artists had made it, maybe even ones he knew. What would it be like to live in a space like this, one that he'd made truly his instead of just somewhere to sleep?

"So what do you think?" Nate asked. "Too déclassé for you?"

I shook my head. "Not at all. I like it."

"Seriously?"

"Yes. My place is luxurious, but yours is relaxing. It suits you."

"You think *you* could be comfortable here? Maybe enough to spend the night?"

Spend the night with Nate? The entire night? My feelings for Nate seemed to be intensifying every day. Could I risk giving him that much of myself?

"Good, then we don't have to rush."

"Wait, I . . ."

Nate smiled. He was torturing me on purpose. "Make yourself at home while I—"

"Slip into something more comfortable?"

Nate laughed. "It's been a long day. I'm in need of a shower."

"So you're going to leave me here to explore."

"You've already figured out my secrets."

"You mean there aren't any more? Because I'd been hoping . . ."

Nate laughed. "Other than the fact that I like you, that your arrogant officiousness turns me on? No, not really."

He shut the door to his bedroom before I could respond to that, not that I had any response except to stare at the door with my mouth open like a complete idiot.

When I'd snapped out of whatever trance his words had put me in, I looked more closely at the art on his walls. Normally, my first instinct would have been to start digging around, because surely he did have other secrets. Usually I wanted to uncover everything I could about people, learn all their weaknesses, but with Nate I didn't need to go through drawers or hack my way into his computer. Now that I'd admitted—to myself at least—that I didn't hate Nate, I had no desire to ruin him. I wanted to find a way to help him succeed, because I liked him, not just for what he did in bed, but for the way he sipped a cocktail, the way he listened so intently, the way he decorated his apartment, and so much more.

I stuck my head into the guest bedroom. It also had an en suite bathroom. There were towels and soap. Maybe I should take a shower too, get all cleaned up before he got me messy. But as soon as I was out of the shower, we were going to fuck. Nate might be able to make me a little less cold and unfeeling, but he wasn't going to make me patient. No one had the power to do that.

Chapter TWELVE

I dried myself and wrapped a towel around my waist. When I stepped out of the guest room, Nate was reclined on the couch wearing bright blue panties that were designed to hold his cock and balls in a little pouch of lace. They were obscene and I was hard in seconds. His lips were red this time. "Not blue to match?" I gestured toward Nate's mouth.

"Would you like that?"

"I . . . Fuck, yeah." I wasn't going to deny it.

"Another time then."

"How many colors of panties do you have?"

"Every color of the rainbow. Eventually, you could see all of them."

"So you don't want to pretend we're not going to do this again?" Why did I ask that? I never asked shit like that.

"Do you?"

"I . . . Let's see how tonight goes."

"Tonight is going to go very well." Nate squared his shoulders, widened his stance, and gave me a haughty smile as he slowly looked me over. I shuddered. Before I tracked him down the other night, I'd only seen his aggressive side when I'd pissed him off in a meeting. It was hot as fuck.

"Is that so?" I asked, needing to challenge him.

"Yes. Drop the towel."

I started to protest, but what was the point? I wanted this and if he wanted to take charge for a while, that was okay. At Kingston I had to be in control, but here, I could let go a little, right? I let the towel hit the floor.

"Now suck me." He shifted so he was sitting up with his legs spread. A smirk on his bright red lips.

I glared at him, and he just laughed.

"You like when I tell you what to do. That's one of your secrets."

"Would you believe me if I told you I've never liked it before?"

"I might because you don't trust easily, and a person needs trust to enjoy this."

"Why should I trust you?"

"You've known me a long time even if you didn't like what I stood for or the way your father interacted with me. You know I'm trustworthy. If you really want me to stop, I will."

He was right, but I wasn't going to give him the satisfaction of saying it. I sank to my knees between his legs. My cock was more than ready for some attention, but I could play his game awhile longer.

I nuzzled the side of his cock and he groaned. As much as I wanted to taste him, part of me hated to unwrap him from the gorgeous blue lace. I looked up and realized that seeing him watching me, eyes dark with lust, was almost as good as watching his pink lips slide along my cock.

Slowly, I peeled the panties down and tucked them under his balls, loving how the fabric framed him for me. I laid my hands on his thighs to steady myself as I ran my tongue over his balls. His thigh muscles went rock hard under my fingers. I kept up the attention until I could hear his short raspy breaths. "Needy?" I asked.

"Fuck, yes."

I smiled at him and gripped the base of his cock, pulling it to my mouth and then sliding my tongue under his head, swirling it back and forth.

He sucked in his breath. "Adam."

Loving the desperation in his voice, I pushed my tongue into the slit.

"Fucking. Fuck."

I smiled up at him and his eyes widened. Then I pulled him deeper and sucked, needing it almost as much as he did. He gripped the side of my head, but I could feel him holding back, which was completely unnecessary. I wanted it rough and dirty.

I gripped his wrists and pulled back.

Nate blinked as if coming out a trance. "Sorry, I—"

"No. That's not why I stopped. I want you to fuck my mouth. I can take it."

"Oh shit."

I slid my hand under the edge of his panties, gripping his ass and jerking him toward me.

He gasped. "You really mean it?"

"Do I look like I'm kidding?"

"Fuck no."

"Okay then."

He took hold of his cock and rubbed it over my lips. "Open up."

I did, tilting my head back so he had a perfect angle.

He thrust into me, almost deep enough to make me gag, before he pulled out and teased me again. I'd never come from being on my knees for a guy before, but Nate just might have made me do it. I liked giving blowjobs, liked seeing how fast I could make a man lose control, but the fact that I was about to lose control myself was completely new and so much better than any sex I'd experienced before.

I rubbed his ass as he worked my mouth, mainly to feel the lace against my hands.

"Look at me," he commanded.

I did, right into his eyes as he drove into my mouth, cock pressing against the back of my throat over and over, and knew I was lost and things were never going to be the same.

Without warning, he stopped and took a step back. His cock was slick with my spit, red and needy, and his hands were actually shaking. I loved how deeply I could affect him, and I wanted more.

"Don't stop."

He shook his head. "Can't go anymore. I . . ."

"Don't you want to come in my mouth?"

He licked his lips. "Oh, God, do I. But not tonight. I'm going to fuck your ass until I have you whimpering and begging, and then I'm going to come buried deep inside you."

His filthy words made my cock jump. "Yeah, that . . . um . . . that sounds good too."

"I know it does."

He shoved his panties down his legs and kicked them off as he pulled me into a kiss that felt like his tongue was fucking my mouth. Our cocks rubbed together and I couldn't keep from thrusting against him.

"Fuck, that's good." He murmured between kisses to my neck. As he licked and bit his way to my collarbone, I imagined the lipstick he was smearing on my throat, and the thought made me even harder. I wrapped a hand around the two of us, but Nate circled my wrist, gripping me hard. "No, I'm too close."

"Scared you can't hold out?"

He glared at me. "I'll make you regret that."

"Try me."

"Oh, I will."

He took my arm and dragged me into his bedroom as he kept kissing me. "Fuck!" He ran into the doorframe and yelped.

"That's what you get for acting like a barbarian."

"You fucking love it."

"Yeah, I do."

"Get on the bed."

I did, positioning myself on all fours. I looked over my shoulder at him. "Do your worst."

"Don't move."

He got the lube and a condom from a dresser drawer, and then he climbed onto the bed. I held my breath in anticipation. This time I wasn't going to fight it. I'd given in to what I needed. I'd let him open me up and push deep inside.

He didn't open the lube like I expected. Instead he pulled my cheeks apart and I felt his hot breath on my ass.

Was he—

He circled my hole with his tongue.

"Holy fuck!"

He laughed and then pushed his tongue into me a little. If he kept it up, I'd come. I wouldn't even need a hand on my cock. I was struggling to believe Nate was actually rimming me. I'd only had one man do that to me before. It had felt good but not—he pushed in again—this oh-my-God amazing.

He held me open for his attentions, groaning like he wanted to tongue my ass as badly as I wanted him to.

A few moments later, I'd had all I could take. "Enough. Please!"

"What's wrong?" He sounded so concerned.

"Nothing." I had to gasp for breath to get any words out. "Nothing's wrong. I . . ."

"You're about to come?"

I nodded frantically.

"Is it hard to hold out? How could that be? The great Adam Kingston can't conquer everything?"

"Bastard."

He wrapped a hand around my cock and balls and squeezed tight, holding back my impending orgasm, and then went back to fucking me with his tongue.

When he stopped several moments later, I felt empty and needy in a way I couldn't ever remember feeling.

I was ready to beg for more attention, but then he entered me with a finger, pushing it deep and sliding over my prostate, forcing an embarrassing squeak from me.

"Good?"

"Shut up."

He chuckled, and I glared at him over my shoulder. "You ready?" he asked.

"More than ready." I couldn't take my eyes off him as he rolled on the condom and slicked his cock.

Nate caressed my ass. "You want to turn over so you can watch?

"No. I want it like this." I actually did want to watch but I'd already let him reduce me to begging. I couldn't let him look into my eyes while he was inside me.

I turned away resting my head on my arm. He laid a hand on my back, and I hated how warm and reassuring it was.

"This is going to be better than anything you've had before."

"We'll see about that." But I knew he was right because what he'd done so far was already better. So very much better. When we weren't arguing, he was almost perfect. I didn't just want him tonight. I wanted him to be part of my life. Oh, fuck, no. That wasn't supposed to happen.

But then Nate pushed into me, slowly, though he never fully stopped. He moved past all my barriers, physical and mental, and I forgot everything then except his cock and my ass.

"You okay?" Nate asked.

I . . . I couldn't pull in enough air to answer. I was so fucking full, but I needed more.

He started to pull out, but I gripped his thigh trying to hold him. "I'm all right, I just . . . need it hard and fast. I don't want to think about anything but fucking."

"Adam—"

"Please."

He drove in and I cried out like before. It felt perfect, burning, hot, like I was going to come apart.

He did it again and again and soon I was driving back to meet him.

"Yes! Like that."

His hands squeezed my hips tightly as he worked in and out. "God, Adam, you're fucking amazing."

"I want you to fucking destroy me."

"Holy shit, Adam. I—"

"Please." I didn't care that I was begging. I just needed him to keep going, to not give me time to panic.

He sat back on his heels and yanked me against him. The new angle made him drag over my sweet spot.

"Oh yes! Oh fuck, yes! I . . . I'm going to fucking come. I can't—"

"No. You're going to wait until I say you can."

"Can't."

"Yes, you can. You will."

"I . . ." Goddamn it! He was right. I would, because I wanted to please him. I would do anything for him.

He yanked me onto his cock and then pushed me off. I gave in and let him control the movement. "That's it. So good, so fucking good."

"Please Nate. Please I need . . . I need you."

"I know, baby, and I'm right here, giving you what you need."

Fuck, he'd called me baby and it almost made me come.

"Hold out a little longer, baby, okay?"

"Yes. No." I tensed as I fought to hold back. He held my hips and thrust, in and out, angling himself to hit my sweet spot. "I can't."

"Yes, you can, just a little longer."

Sweat dripped from my face and chest. I bit my lips, fighting . . . fighting . . .

"You can come now."

Oh, God. My entire body lit up as heat gathered in my balls. My legs tingled, my breath caught and then—

"Yes! Nate!" I shouted as I came and then sagged against the mattress. He'd destroyed me just like I'd asked.

He came right after me, driving hard into my ass. I winced, the thrusts hurt, but I wouldn't mind that aching reminder of what we'd done.

A few seconds later, he pulled out and I rolled away. I couldn't look at him, couldn't think, but then he was there again, running a hand up and down my back. "Do you want me here or do you need time alone?"

"I think I should go, or maybe . . ." Did I really want to be alone? My heart was racing and I couldn't catch my breath. If only it was just the amazing orgasm, but it wasn't. I wished I could explain it but no words would come. I curled in on myself.

"Just nod if you want me to go in another room and leave you alone."

How could he want me here when I was such a freak, so incapable of this connection? I didn't want him to leave. I wanted him to hold me, wanted his warm body pressed against mine. It terrified me to need someone like that, but I refused to give into that fear.

I snuggled closer as I reached back and laid my hand over his. "Stay," I whispered. And he did, spooning against me. We fell asleep like that.

We dozed for a few hours. Then I jerked us both off as we kissed. He was the best fucking kisser.

The next time I woke the sun was shining in my eyes. I couldn't believe how late I'd slept. I turned over to wake Nate but he wasn't there. Why hadn't he woken me?

I stumbled to his bathroom. When I'd showered, I realized my clothes were in the other bedroom, the same clothes I'd worn the day before. Great. I was going to have to go home before I went to the office.

I wandered into his living area in a towel.

"Good morning," Nate said. His bright smile was disgustingly cheerful.

"Um . . ."

"I'm making pancakes. I called Brad and let him know you'd be in later."

Oh, fuck. What else had he said?

"Don't worry. I just told him we were meeting over breakfast. But I figured we could just work here."

Making pancakes? Work here? Like lovers cozied up after a night together. A montage of Nate and me flashed in my mind as if we were starring in a rom-com. Him making dinner. Me taking him out to my favorite club. Us on vacation together. Dating. In a relationship. Me out as bi. My chest ached. Those scenes made up a beautiful fantasy, but it wasn't one I could have, because I wasn't cut out for relationships. The night before, Nate had helped me accept comfort and warmth from him, but if we stayed together, that wouldn't last. No one would want to spend that much time with me day after day.

My lovers never asked me to spend the night, and no one had ever made me breakfast. That kind of domesticity was for other people.

My hands began to tingle, and I grabbed the back of a chair to steady myself. My panic last night had been bad enough. I couldn't let Nate see how his presence was getting to me in the light of day. "No, we're not working here after . . . whatever this was. I need to go home."

"What's wrong?" Nate frowned and started to move around the corner.

Did I sound as frantic as I felt? *Act normal.* "I don't do morning-afters. I'm going to run by my apartment. I'll be in the office in an hour."

Nausea tightened my throat when I saw the hurt in his eyes. "Adam, I thought . . ."

I squeezed the chair tighter. "What?"

Nate held my gaze a few seconds, then shook his head. "Never mind."

He looked so fucking disappointed. I almost relented, but I had to stay distant or I was going to lose it completely. My heart was pounding hard now and my chest was getting tight. Was I going to pass out? *Please let me hold it together long enough to get dressed and call Darryl.* Where was my fucking phone anyway? Maybe I'd left it in my pants in the guest room.

I forced myself to take slow steps. When I found my phone, it was showing ten messages: three from Valerie, two from Brad, and the rest from various people at Kingston.

I called Valerie first, standing there naked, hands shaking, world darkening at the edges. Was I going to lose it completely? Maybe giving the company to Nate was the right decision, after all.

"Adam, are you ok?" Valerie asked.

"Yes. No."

"Where are you?"

"At Nate's."

"Really?"

"Yes. But I've got to get out of here." I was pulling on my pants as I talked to her.

"I'm in my car," Valerie said. "I'll have my driver come by. What's the address?"

"I . . . Fuck, I don't know, but Darryl can find out. I'll have him get me."

"Is Nate there?"

"Yes." I picked up my shirt.

"You could ask him."

"No, I . . . I don't think he wants to talk to me anymore." I switched the phone to my opposite hand so I could put my arm through the other sleeve.

"Adam, what happened?"

"We fucked. It was great. Then he made me pancakes and I panicked and treated him like an ass."

"Ah. I see."

"No, I don't think—"

"Adam, I do understand."

"Fine, whatever, but I've got to get the hell out of here and then figure out how to face him in the office."

"And tonight?" she asked.

"I'll go home and sulk."

She sighed. "Right. Shall I join you?"

"No, I want to sulk alone." I said as I buttoned my shirt.

"You sure that's a good idea?"

I tucked my shirt in and looked around for my socks. "Yes." *No.* "I've got to go, okay?"

Valerie sighed. "Don't hurt him."

"What about me?"

"Adam."

"I've got to go." I ended the call, buttoned my shirt, and tucked it in.

After I'd called Darryl, I pulled on my jacket and stuffed my phone and tie into the pocket as I pushed my feet into my shoes.

"I'll see you at the office," I called as I breezed past Nate, trying to look preoccupied.

Nate looked up from his plate of pancakes. It didn't look like he'd eaten more than a few bites. "Why are you doing this?"

"Because . . ." *I'm terrified.* "We need to focus on work now."

I stood in the doorway for a few seconds. The pain and confusion in Nate's expression made my chest ache, and every part of me screamed that I was making a huge mistake. But the fear that was making my hands shake wouldn't let me stay, so I stepped over the threshold and closed the door behind me.

Chapter
THIRTEEN

"Mr. Thomas is here, sir," Brad announced.

"Send him in." Several hours had passed since I'd left his apartment, and I'd been pacing my office waiting for him to show up so we could hash through the details of the plan he'd outlined the night before.

When Nate stepped through the door, I kept my eyes on the papers in front of me. "I've got some ideas about how best to pull this off."

"Then explain them."

I'd expected him to try to get me to talk about how I'd run him off. But, I'd never seen him so cold. I'd fucked up, but I had no idea in hell how to fix it.

We worked through a few points of contention. Nate was polite but he never warmed up.

Wasn't this best, though? A professional relationship. No more fucking. No more making it all personal, too personal, causing me to feel . . . Fuck, no it wasn't better. I was empty inside.

I'd thought so, but the idea of losing Nate, of facing years of cold, polite meetings, scared me more than the idea of a relationship.

But what could I say? I sucked at apologies. If I tried, the wrong thing would come out of my mouth.

Because you're selfish and never think you're wrong.

My chest tightened. I became dizzy, nauseous. I was wrong this time. I should've talked to him.

I heard Val's sensible voice whispering to me: *It's okay to panic, but you need to apologize and admit that you need help with your anxiety.*

I'm the CTO of a global conglomerate. I don't have time for panic attacks.

That's funny, because you're having them.

Nate tapped the screen of his tablet. "We should have our marketing team work on rebranding our Entertainment division. Our target market has shifted and we need a fresh ad campaign."

"I like that idea."

Nate simply nodded and moved on down his list. *Damn.* I'd hoped agreeing with him might thaw him out a bit. Maybe, instead, a rousing argument would stir things up. I'd rather have him angry than cold.

Nate was looking at the next point. "To prove *I* know how to compromise, I'll agree to eliminate a quarter of the research staff in the Enviro division and roll the others into a dedicated team in Corporate Research."

"No, half need to go at least."

Nate shook his head. "I've got recommendations for low performers and employees close to retirement age. Those account for close to a quarter of my staff. The others are essential."

I ignored him. "Your staff isn't essential if we have people in Research who can do their jobs."

"You don't. My staff knows our business intimately. They are best qualified to tweak our products as we move into new markets."

"How do you know? Have you actually studied my researchers' skills?"

"I'm not laying more people off."

"Are you going to pay them out of your own pocket? There's no budget for them."

"Then we need to cut something else."

"What? You don't seem willing to cut anything."

"I suggested other cuts a few minutes ago, and I'm agreeing to cut ten people from my division."

"Ten isn't going to do it. Besides you'll no doubt want to offer them packages that will break us."

He glared at me. "I am willing to use the standard package Kingston offers."

"Do that for half your research staff and we're good."

"Adam, I don't know what the fuck your problem is. If you're taking out your anger at me on my employees—"

"I'm doing business. I'm being realistic."

"You're being a fucking ass."

I slammed my hand down on my desk. "Someone has to be. You can't make fucking sunshine and rainbows out of this."

"Do you really think that's what we're doing? I don't think you have a clue how hard I work. How hard my people work."

"I suppose it takes a lot of effort to dream up impossible schemes to save the world?"

Nate shoved his tablet in to his bag. "Fuck you, Adam. When you're ready to actually work let me know. Until then, I'll be in the lab talking to my people about something that might both help the world and make us money, because contrary to what you think, the two are not mutually exclusive."

No, but hating someone and fucking them apparently is.

You do not hate Nate.

No I . . . I love him. Oh fuck no. I'm not supposed to think that. I can't.

Nate opened the door. *Are you going to let him walk away?*

"Wait. I'll talk now . . ."

Nate turned back, brows raised. "You'll consider realistic proposals?"

"Yes. I . . . I'm sorry."

The shock on his face was too much. Did he really think I couldn't apologize?

Don't you?

I was like the walking dead for the rest of the afternoon. But I kept working on the plan. Several times I called in some people from other divisions for consultations. And even though Nate didn't seem to notice that I was actually taking other people's advice, just having someone else in the room allowed me to breathe more easily. The tension radiating between me and Nate was slowly strangling me. Yet, I couldn't stop myself from watching him work. My stomach fluttered every time I thought about what I really wanted from Nate. Companionship. Intimacy. What would it be like to actually have a partner, not just in business, but in life?

During the remainder of the afternoon, Nate gave in on a few things. I gave in more than I ever have in my life, but he remained distant, professional but with none of the passion I was used to seeing in him.

That evening I lay on my bed staring at the ceiling. I hadn't eaten all day, but I didn't feel hungry. Part of me wanted to get drunk, though another part of me knew I'd be sick after a few drinks, not to mention I'd been drinking too much lately. So I stayed there, almost in a trance. Thinking and not thinking. Seeing my future self: bitter, hostile, alone, arguing every point with Nate, with the board, until I hated Kingston Corp. and wanted to leave.

I didn't want that to happen. I loved my company, even if I only knew how to show it by fighting.

What had my father said? That I needed to learn how to be a different man than the one he raised, that I had to learn to compromise, to see other people's perspective, that I needed to do better than he had. That between Nate and me we could fix everything because of our differences, not despite them.

But what the hell did he know? The cruel bastard couldn't even manage a relationship with his own son.

Ten days had passed since I'd run out on Nate. We'd presented our progress to the board and they'd made some suggestions, most of which I hated. Otherwise, I'd managed to avoid being in the same room with him. We'd mainly communicated through texts and emails since conveniently, he'd visited a customer in LA, and I'd spent the last two days in our New York office, trying to make the lab manager understand how to meet Kingston's standards. That hadn't gone well, and I'd been left in a shitty mood. Usually when I felt like this and Valerie was in town, we ate pizza and got stinking drunk.

Tonight she was at the opera, so she wouldn't be available for hours. The worse thing was I didn't want to talk to her anyway. I wanted to talk to Nate. I hated the coldness between us since I proved exactly how unfit I am to have a relationship. Morning-after panic attacks must be a deal breaker.

If you'd told him how you were feeling, admitted how serious your anxiety was, maybe it wouldn't be.

I could imagine trying to start that conversation. *I'm Adam Kingston and I panic when offered pancakes.*

But I really fucking missed him. He was the first thing I thought about when I woke up and images of him filled my dreams. I'd happily go back to the old days of nonstop arguing just to have him around. Now that we were barely speaking, I thought of things to tell him multiple times a day. I even had pretend conversations with him in my mind and imagined his responses. How had he become so important to me? We'd argued for weeks, had dinner once, and fucked two times, which didn't seem like enough to change our relationship, but I felt like I'd lost one of my closest friends.

So go get him.

No. I'd hurt him and there were a hundred other reasons we would never work. He was out while I was still hiding, and I'd yet to figure out how to relax enough around him to do anything other than argue or fuck. And if we tried to date and things blew up, it could spell the end of Kingston. It wasn't worth the risk, was it?

Yes.

No.

You've always been a risk taker.

Not this time.

I closed my eyes and saw nothing but Nate. Fuck. If I really was too much of a coward to give us another chance, I was going to have to do something to purge Nate from my mind.

Getting drunk would only leave me feeling worse. But a good fuck wouldn't. Maybe that was exactly what I needed.

Darryl was waiting for me when I landed at O'Hare. "Home, Mr. Kingston?"

"No. Remember the club you took me to when I needed to find Mr. Thomas?" Why the hell had I forgotten the name of it?

"Yes, sir."

"I'd like you to take me there."

"Are you sure, sir? You must be tired and hungry. I could order you some food, and it would arrive by the time we got to your apartment."

I sighed. "I appreciate you trying to take care of me, but I'm going to the club. Ass-some. That's the name."

Darryl nodded. "Yes, sir. I'll take you wherever you want to go. Are you meeting Mr. Thomas again?"

"No." I didn't elaborate and it wasn't his place to ask. "Let me off a few blocks away and wait for me there."

Darryl frowned, but he simply said, "Yes, sir."

Once I was settled in the car, Darryl closed my door, took his seat, and pulled out into traffic.

Of course, Nate might be there. I wasn't privy to his schedule, and I'd sworn I'd never invade his privacy by stalking him again. Plus the last thing I wanted was to see him grinding up on some other man, because then I'd want . . . No, I wasn't going there for him. I simply wanted to find a man to fuck the awful day away.

If wanting to hide your bisexuality is a reason not to go after Nate, what are you doing heading to a club where anyone could see you?

I hated that pretentious voice in my head. *No one there cares who I am.*

Are you so sure?

I wasn't, but I wouldn't let fear keep me from my mission.

Maybe a little fear is healthy.

Or a little risk.

Shut the fuck up.

Darryl pulled up to the curb down the street from the club, then came around to my door to let me out, promising to wait close by. Once I was inside, I ordered a drink. I needed alcohol to help me remember exactly why I was there.

To do something supremely stupid.

To enjoy myself and get laid. Maybe a hard dirty bathroom fuck would break the constant loop of Nate thoughts in my head.

I finished my drink, hung my jacket over a chair, and made my way on to the dance floor.

I was dancing with a hot dangerously young blond who'd untucked my shirt so he could run his hands over my back when I saw Nate. His lipstick was blue. That was supposed to be for me. Was he wearing the matching panties? The bastard.

I slithered out of the boy's clutches, done dancing for the moment. *I'm not seeking out Nate. No, I'm definitely not.* I needed another drink to strengthen my resolve.

I ordered two shots of tequila, the perfect big-mistake drink. I threw one back followed rapidly by the next. Someone grabbed my arm as I was sucking the lime slice.

It was Nate.

I pulled away from him. "Get your hands off me."

"Adam, you're not thinking clearly."

I snorted. "And you are? If you can troll for tricks here, so can I."

"Adam." He frowned at the shot glasses on the bar. "How many of these have you had?"

"Not enough. I can still see you."

Nate shook his head. "Don't be stupid, Adam. Let me call you a cab?"

"Fuck no. You don't get to cockblock me."

Nate moved closer and this time I let him be in my space. "For your information, I just came here to dance."

"Riiight." I signaled the bartender. I needed another shot if I was going to have to listen to lies.

Nate shook his head at the bartender, and the man turned to another customer.

"I need a drink."

"No, you don't. And I'm not lying. I haven't been with anyone since you."

I sneered at him. "Is that a record?"

"Ha! So you really came here looking for a fuck tonight?"

"Yes. And if you're not going to find someone for me, then leave me alone so I can get on with it."

He took my arm again, dragged me toward the back of the club, and pulled me into a dim hallway. Several couples were already there, taking advantage of the semi-privacy.

Nate glanced around.

"Who are you looking for?" I asked. "Are you like my pimp now?"

"No, I'm the man who's going to give you what you need."

"B-but—" I sputtered.

"Shut up."

I took a swing at him, but he grabbed my arm, twisted it behind my back, and pushed me face first against the wall. I'd never been so turned on in my life.

He teased the outside of my ear with his tongue. "Is this what you want? An anonymous fuck with your face scraping a cinder block wall, exposed where anyone could see you?"

I licked my suddenly dry lips. "Yes."

"You want me to fuck you with no care for whether it hurts you. You want me to push you to your knees, make you suck my cock."

"I . . ." I was so fucking hard I couldn't think.

"You want to fuck and then forget it happened, to ignore what you need and who you are after you leave this club?"

"I . . . I don't—"

"Shut up. That was a rhetorical question."

I thought he was going to walk away. Surely he wouldn't actually fuck me here like this, would he?

A moment later, I got my answer when he reached around, unfastened my jeans, and shoved them over my hips.

Eager for more, I widened my stance. If he was game, so was I.

A slurping sound had me glancing over my shoulder. Nate had two fingers in his mouth and was coating them thoroughly with spit. He used his other hand to push my face back against the wall.

"Don't look. You're not supposed to see me, remember? Just feel me in your ass."

"Oh fuck."

"Yes!" He leaned in close, mouth touching my ear. "You do want this, don't you?"

I nodded. "God, yes."

"Good. Then open up for me."

He slid his wet fingers down my crack and entered me. He wasn't as rough as I'd expected, but he wasn't gentle either. I managed not to flinch or cry out as he began to finger fuck me.

"Relax," he ordered.

I pushed back, taking his fingers deeper even as I thought: *This can't be happening.*

It was, though, and I fucking loved it, no matter how much my mind tried to tell me I shouldn't.

He ripped open a condom packet. "You ready now?"

"Yes!" I barely got the word out before he thrust into me, and I had to press my lips together to hold in a shout.

"Fuck you're tight. Feels so good."

His breath was hot on my neck. I groaned and tilted my head to the side.

He took the invitation, licking the drops of sweat running down my neck and then biting as he drove in again.

I cried out.

He covered my mouth with one of his hands, the other holding my hip, keeping me in place for his harsh strokes. "Can't have you making too much noise back here."

I fought to drag in enough air through my nose as I pushed back against him, wanting more. He fucked me relentlessly. I struggled at first, fighting what I wanted. Then I just gave in and let him.

Eventually, he took his hand off my mouth. "Keep quiet even when I make you come."

I nodded. *Please don't stop.*

He wrapped that hand around my cock and jacked me to the same rhythm as his thrusts. I reveled in the sensation of his body pressed against mine, heating every inch of me. When I dragged in a breath, his scent overpowered me. I leaned into the wall, giving him complete control. He was everything I wanted.

I braced my forehead against my hand barely able to stay upright. My balls drew up tight and lightning sizzled through my body as orgasm seized me. I bit down on the fleshy part below my thumb as I shot over Nate's fingers.

"Fuck," Nate gasped and he jerked against my ass as he came too.

"Yeah." I stayed still for several seconds, enjoying the post-sex stupor. Then Nate pulled out.

"Goodbye, Adam," he whispered against my ear.

I stood there with my hand throbbing, the cool of the wall against my face doing nothing to ease the heat pouring off me . . . I already missed the feel of Nate against my back, his warmth, the way he obviously wanted me as badly as I wanted him.

Nate's word finally sank into my addled mind. He'd said *"Goodbye."*

I found the energy to push away from the wall and pull up my pants. When I turned around, I scanned the area for Nate, hoping he might not have gone far. No such luck. He'd left me there. Alone, with a throbbing ass and what was surely a bite mark on my neck. I stepped back into the main area of the club and forced myself to head toward the door rather than searching for him there. So this had been a farewell fuck? Fine. I wasn't chasing him.

I called Darryl, which wasn't easy with my hands shaking.

"Are you all right, sir?" he asked.

"I'm fine, just ready to go home now."

"Yes, sir."

I wasn't fine. I was about to lose it right there. What the hell had I done?

After what seemed like an endless drive though traffic, Darryl dropped me at the front door of my building. He wanted to walk me up, but I told him I hardly needed a bodyguard in a posh building like mine.

"No, sir, but you don't seem to be feeling well."

"I'm fine. Thank you though." I needed to be in my own space, alone, where I could fall apart.

I couldn't sleep, I lay in my bed.

"Goodbye, Adam." The words echoed in my mind.

It wasn't like I'd never see Nate again. He'd be there at Kingston whether I liked it or not. But to never touch him again, never kiss him again— Is that what he'd meant? Is that what he wanted or did I still have a chance? If I listened to Nate, if I admitted that I needed him, could that possibly be enough to make him trust me?

My father hadn't, and I'd rarely trusted myself.

I don't have any idea how to be part of a team. That's not what I'm cut out for. I should be researching in the lab. I . . .

Shouldn't be the CEO . . .

Maybe that was the key.

I grabbed my laptop and began typing furiously. We had another progress meeting with the board the next day. Maybe I could still show Nate I cared, after all.

Chapter
FOURTEEN

*T*he next day at work I didn't attempt to communicate with Nate at all. I focused completely on what I had to do, even though it made my stomach flutter. I was determined to appear calm and collected at the meeting.

I'd timed my entrance so I'd be just a few minutes late. Once I thought everyone would be there, I headed down the hall and pushed open the boardroom door.

When I entered, Nate's expression filled with anger, uncertainty, maybe even pain. But I couldn't think about that now.

I can do this.

"I have an announcement." No one was shocked when I interrupted one of the board members.

Marsha glared at me. "This better be good."

"It is."

Now Nate just looked angry. "We didn't discuss—"

"We don't need to discuss this."

"Adam."

"I want to retain my position as CTO after the transition, rather than taking joint control with Nate."

"What?" Nate and Marsha spoke simultaneously. The rest of the board stared.

"I know my father intended for me to take over as CEO and a position of president to be created for Nate, but I don't think that will work."

Everyone remained silent, so I continued.

"Marsha, I'd like you to take the CFO position. Martin doesn't want to work with me or Nate since he's considering retiring, so let's send him on his way at the end of the year."

"Adam, what's going on?" Nate asked.

"My strengths lie in technology development, not in being CEO. Nate, you're much better with people; you'll be a great CEO. I want you to have the position."

"But you said—"

"I'm not giving up my share of the company. I'll still be an owner, but I don't want—"

"You're saying you're going to listen to what I want for the company? That I'm going to make executive decisions?"

"I expect to be consulted like anyone else on the executive team, but yes."

"Your father wanted—"

I held up my hand. "What he wanted was for us to use our talents to help Kingston. This is the best way for us to do that. It's a compromise that can actually work." At least I hoped to hell it was.

"Nate, are you willing to take sole responsibility as CEO?" Marsha asked, redirecting us.

Nate looked at me. I couldn't read him at all now. Was he going to protest?

"Yes, I agree to Adam's suggestion."

With a long exhale, I sank into a chair, trying to hide my shaking hands, hardly hearing the rest of the meeting. I must have agreed or argued as expected, because no one prompted me to do otherwise.

When Marsha called an end to the proceedings, I gathered my things and headed for the door, hoping I could slip out before Nate cornered me.

I only made it as far as the elevator before he caught up.

"What the fuck, Adam?"

I forced a smile as I stepped into the elevator and hit the button for my floor. "It's best for both of us. I thought you'd be happy."

Nate followed me. "I don't know what to think. Yes, objectively it's the best decision, so I agreed to it. But I . . . just need to know that you're not going to come back in a few weeks and decide to fight me about everything. I can't be CEO if you're constantly challenging me."

"Do you actually think I'm that much of an asshole?"

Nate glared at me.

"I'm not going back on what I said. I won't be challenging you, not for the position anyway."

"I don't suppose I could get that in writing?"

"Wow, you really trust me, don't you?" The elevator doors opened, and I stepped out onto my floor, not waiting for a reply. Once again Nate followed.

I'd actually thought he'd be ready to forgive me, that my gesture would be enough to at least get him to look at me instead of through me. When we reached my office, I opened the door and motioned for him to come in.

"How about we discuss it over dinner?" I asked as we entered my office.

"Dinner?" He stared at me like I was batshit crazy.

"Yes."

"And then back to your place for sex?"

"I ... Well, sure if that's what you want."

"Are you fucking serious?"

The tightness in my chest made it hard to breathe. I never expected him to sound so angry and bitter.

"You think just because you did something good for Kingston I'm going to forget the other morning or whatever and do your bidding again."

Had I really blown my chance with him? "What's your problem, Nate? I'm sorry I was an asshole, okay? I freaked out yesterday morning. I'm not the best at staying the night."

"My problem is that you're way too used to getting whatever you want. Has anyone ever said no to you?"

"Yes." I thought about that for a second. "My father. Probably plenty of others." Though I couldn't think of any.

He snorted. "Probably *not*. You have no idea how to handle rejection or anything not going your way."

"Nate, I said I was sorry. For God's sake, I gave up control of the company so—"

"So I'd fuck you again or fall under your spell? This is just another bribe."

"No, I'm doing what's right for Kingston, but I also hoped—"

"Then you're a fool. You can't buy me with compromise any more than with money. I'm not going to bow down to you because you did something reasonable for once. I may care about people, but I'm not a pushover."

"Yeah, I got that." He'd made that clear when we'd fucked.

We both looked away then. Nate gazed out the window and I stared at the papers on my desk. The figures seeming to swirl and dance.

"I just wanted you to talk to me again."

Nate whirled to face me, for just a moment, his expression softened, but then he shook his head. "I'm not sure there's a point in talking. I tried to open up to you, to see if you could drop your front and be a real person with me, even after you intruded on my personal life, even after you threatened me with my secrets."

"I told you that was a mistake. I would never have followed through. I—"

"I believed you. I guess I still do, but I let you in on my secrets. I shared them with you, dressed up for you, and then you walked out on me and—"

"Nate, you don't understand."

He walked to the window and leaned his head against it. "Yeah, I do. You took what you wanted, but you didn't want to face the consequences. You're so caught up in putting up the front of Adam Kingston the Great—cold, selfish, straight man—that you couldn't handle the idea of what I made you feel."

"Look, I can't—"

He turned back to face me, hands fisted. "Let me finish. I'm fucking sick of you controlling everything."

"I didn't dominate when we—"

"This isn't about how you act in bed."

I sank into my desk chair. "No, it's about us."

"According to you, there is no us."

"Maybe I was wrong about that."

Nate shook his head. "You think you can't be the same person at work and in private, so you can fuck me and then lord it over me here."

"Is that what just happened? Because I must have gone to a completely different meeting."

Nate crossed the room and braced his arms on my desk. As much as I wanted to, I couldn't look away from him. "What just happened is you discarded me from your personal life and then thought I'd be happy to step right back in again."

"Do you really think that's how I feel?"

"Yes." Nate's tone was as cold as his eyes.

"Then get the fuck out of my office."

Nate slammed the door and walked away.

I dropped my head into my hands and quit fighting the tears that stung my eyes.

I went to the Imperial when I left work, but quickly realized I didn't want to be around anyone, especially not cute, flirtatious waiters and happy couples drinking together. I went home, went to bed, tossed and turned, hating Nate, hating myself. Hating that what I'd done might be enough for Kingston but it wasn't enough for Nate and me. Finally, close to dawn, I took a sleeping pill and crashed.

I woke to my phone blaring Valerie's ring. I squinted at the time.

"What time is it?" I said into the phone.

"It's a good thing I'm used to your rude way of answering, Adam. It's three. In the afternoon."

"Huh. I didn't think I'd sleep that long."

"When did you go to bed?"

"Around 6 a.m."

"Were you with Nate?"

The excitement in her voice made my stomach knot. "No chance of that." Our conversation in my office started replaying in my head for the millionth time.

"Didn't the meeting go well?"

"The meeting?"

She huffed. "The board meeting? You texted me that you had a great plan. Did they like it?"

"Oh, yeah. They did," I said.

"You don't sound very excited."

I didn't have the energy to explain more right then. "I'm not very awake."

"We haven't had hot dogs in the park yet this visit. Meet me there at five?"

Maybe by then I'd be able to talk about last night. Maybe I'd actually be proud of my decision again. "I'll be there."

I ended the call and dragged myself from the bed and headed to the shower. It wasn't like I'd get back to sleep anyway.

Chapter
FIFTEEN

*V*alerie showed up wearing a gorgeous velvet gown and glittering red heels.

Before I could comment, she said, "I'm going to the ballet with my sister-in-law in a few hours. I didn't want to go back and change."

"I can't think of anything I'd rather wear to eat a hot dog in."

She looked me up and down. "Blue would suit you better."

I rolled my eyes and gestured toward a park bench. "Have a seat. I'll be right back."

Once I'd obtained two fully loaded dogs and two sodas, I settled on the bench next to Valerie. She covered her lap in napkins and enjoyed a few bites before she said, "So tell me what happened at the meeting."

I decided to start with my plan for Kingston. At least that was easier than explaining that Nate still hated me. "I got back from New York and knew I had to think of something, because if things kept on as they were, Kingston would only get sicker . . ."

"That sounds promising. What's your plan?"

"I told Nate he should have sole control of Kingston. I'm much better suited to the CTO position. It's where I belong."

Valerie tilted her head and tapped her fingers on her leg for a few seconds, then she nodded. "I agree."

"Marsha is going to step in as CFO at the end of the year. She will enact the plan Nate and I developed, and with her to curb Nate's spending and me to temper his idealism and push him to consider the needs of all the businesses, I think we can save Kingston."

Valerie smiled. "You can, because you'll be working together. I'm proud of you. Your father would be too."

I sighed. "I always thought I'd be running things."

She laid her hand on my thigh. "It's your company no matter what position you hold."

"Mine and Nate's."

She nodded.

Squeezing her hand, I said, "So you really think I made the right decision?"

"Yes."

I sighed. "It sure as hell wasn't easy admitting to everyone I shouldn't be CEO . . ."

Valerie smiled. "I bet not. You shouldn't think of it that way though. You're the finest fucking CTO they'll ever have. If you leave that position, things will go to shit."

I laughed. "That does sounds more like me."

"It's okay to be you as long as you know your strengths and weaknesses."

"I've had to consider my weaknesses more than I ever wanted to these past few weeks."

"Then as cruel as it was of your father to write those words rather than say them himself, he gave you exactly what you needed."

I shrugged. "Maybe."

"Now what about Nate?"

I shrugged. "What about him? In time, I'm sure he'll be thrilled to be CEO."

"No, I mean what about you and Nate."

"Me and Nate? There's no me and Nate."

"The fact that you fucked him would say otherwise."

I rolled my eyes. Beautiful Valerie in her beautiful dress eating a hot dog and spouting obscenities was one of my favorite things in the world.

"You care about him."

She clearly wasn't going to let this go. "He doesn't want anything to do with me now."

"You hurt him, didn't you?"

I nodded. "And I don't know how to fix it."

"You want to fix it, though."

"I do. And . . ."

Valerie leaned closer. "Yes?"

"It's not just sex. I think I might be in love with him."

Valerie's eyes widened. "Well, that is progress."

"It's hell is what it is, because I finally made him hate me. I went to a club after I got back to town the other night. Nate was there."

"And . . ."

Heat rose to my face as I remembered it. "It was a hate fuck."

Valerie grinned. "You liked it?"

"Maybe, but he made it clear afterwards that he didn't want anymore to do with me."

"He's going to regret that, and you will too if you just let him go. You've changed and I think he's the right man for you. Besides, who else but me is willing to stand up to your nonsense?"

I rolled my eyes. "Just because Nate had no problem telling me off—"

"He doesn't put up with your bullshit. That's what you need."

"I have no idea how to win him back. He thinks I ran out on him."

"Just talk to him. Be open and honest. He's a smart man, and I bet he can tell the difference between honesty and blustering."

"I tried to talk to him, but he kept yelling at me, saying all I care about is myself."

"There are times he'd have a point."

"This wasn't one of them. He thinks I ran out on him deliberately the other morning, but I didn't. I panicked. I couldn't breathe. I thought I'd make a fool of myself."

"Not realizing that running away was worse?"

I rubbed my neck, trying to ease the tight muscles. "I protected myself. Maybe I am just selfish."

"No, you're not. You were scared, and you didn't know how to handle that. It's okay to feel that way."

"But he wouldn't let me explain."

"He was angry. Did you acknowledge that he had a right to be?"

"No, but I'm ready to now."

Valerie nodded. "Good."

Could I do what she suggested, be open? Could I tell Nate why I'd run that morning and make him understand how much I cared?

I grabbed my phone and called him.

"Hello?"

"Nate, I'm sorry I was an ass. I want to see you." I didn't dare look at Valerie. If I was screwing this up, I didn't want to know.

"You do?"

"Yeah. Would you come over tonight? Whatever time works for you?"

"Adam, I don't—"

"Please. Just give me a chance to explain why I've been such an asshole." God, it hurt to beg like that.

"Okay. I'll be there at eight."

"Thanks. See you then."

"Adam?"

I'd been about to end the call, but I put the phone back to my ear. "Yeah?"

"I'm sorry about the night at the club."

"It's okay. It was actually . . ." I glanced at Valerie, but she was focused on her hot dog. "Fucking hot."

"Yeah, but I shouldn't have left."

"That's the role you were playing and I deserved it."

"No, you didn't. You really didn't."

"Thanks. For saying that." Wow. I sounded like an idiot. "See you tonight."

"Yeah." Nate ended the call.

"So he agreed? You're seeing him later?"

I nodded, wishing I were as excited as Valerie.

"Excellent."

"Maybe." I wouldn't know until he was there, and I had no idea what to do or say and only a few hours to figure it out.

"I believe in you. You'll get Nate and you'll turn Kingston around. And if you need anything, a loan or—"

I shook my head. "You've done plenty. You don't have to be my benefactress just yet. I've got plenty of savings, and we're going to turn this around."

"Yes, you will." She hugged me tightly, and as I relaxed into the embrace, most of my tension drained away.

A few moments later, she kissed my cheek and stepped back. "Now go get ready for your date."

Chapter
SIXTEEN

As I walked home, it occurred to me that Nate might be staying late at the office and wouldn't have eaten dinner. I could suggest we go out but . . . Nate liked doing things like regular people rather than rich executives. Regular people ate at home, right? I didn't have time to cook and besides, I might burn the building down. But I could pick up something and set the table. I had nice dishes somewhere. Maybe even a tablecloth. What else? Flowers. I should get flowers for the table.

It didn't take me long to acquire a bouquet from a street vendor— Nate would appreciate that they were wildflowers not hothouse ones, right?—and food from a Greek deli down the street from my apartment. I wouldn't likely be hungry after my hot dogs but hopefully Nate would like my choices. Had I ever wanted to please someone as much as I did Nate that night?

I sat the food down on the counter. First I needed a vase for the flowers. Where would a vase be? Did I own a vase? I must because my housekeeper left flowers on the table sometimes. One of the lower cabinets yielded a choice of three vases. I chose a cut glass one, filled it with water, and stuck the flowers in it. They flopped over, but I didn't have time to worry over them.

Plates next. I knew where the everyday ones were. I did occasionally heat up leftovers for myself. But the nicer ones . . .

I opened cabinet after cabinet before finally remembering the hutch in the dining room. That's where they were.

Now a tablecloth. A thorough search left me empty-handed. Hmmm. What was the difference between a white sheet and a tablecloth? Not much really. Maybe in low light Nate wouldn't notice.

I checked the clock. I had thirty minutes left, plenty of time to set the table and change into something nicer. Of course, I still had no idea what to say.

I flung the sheet over the table. It looked . . . like a sheet. What the hell? I might as well leave it. I already needed to confess to having panic attacks, a desire for Nate that went beyond lust—no way in hell was I using the L word—and apologize. What was one more embarrassing thing?

I set a place for Nate and one for me. I had to at least have a bite of the spanakopita. It smelled amazing. I put the flowers in the center of the table and then spread the food out along the counter so Nate could make choices and fill his own plate. I raced to the bedroom.

When I was dressed, I glanced at the clock. Five minutes to go now.

The buzzer made me jump. He was early. Oh fuck. I didn't have a plan except begging him not to give up on me. Would that even work?

I opened the door. Nate was wearing shorts, plaid ones, and a faded light blue shirt with the sleeves rolled up.

"I guess I'm overdressed," I said, feeling self-conscious. "I've worn suits so long I don't remember how to do casual."

He looked me over. "Did you go to one of those prep schools where you wear suits to class?"

"Guilty as charged."

"Well." He seemed to consider his words carefully. "I like you in suits."

I like you in anything.

I smiled and then a bit of nervous laughter relaxed me enough to help me remember to step back and gesture for him to enter.

His eyes widened when he saw the table. "You did this? For me?"

"I know it's not quite right, but . . ."

Nate shook his head. "It's . . ." He circled the room, studying it carefully. "Is that a bed sheet?"

"Umm . . . yes. I wanted to do it myself instead of hiring someone. I wanted you to know it was . . . me. That I . . ."

"Adam."

"I ordered some food." If I kept the conversation going maybe he wouldn't have time to decide he didn't want to be here.

"It smells great."

"It's Greek. I got all vegetarian stuff. I didn't know if you ate lamb."

"Adam, I—"

"I need to explain some things," I blurted out. "Things that aren't easy for me to say. Things no one but Valerie—and my fucking therapist—know."

"If you're embarrassed about seeing a therapist—"

"Not embarrassed, just pissed off that I need one."

"You don't have time for such petty problems?"

His words would've infuriated me a few weeks ago. Now, I knew he was teasing. "Something like that."

"Does this have to do with why you ran out on me?"

"You had every right to be angry. I was an ass. I usually am. Valerie says I have no idea how to apologize because I've never been made to."

"And now you're trying to apologize?"

"Yes. Am I doing it right?"

"No one has ever sacrificed their sheets so I could eat a meal in style before, so I think so."

"I have panic attacks," I blurted the words out because I'd chicken out if I waited. "They started when my father was ill and I realized how bad things really were with Kingston's financials. I've had anxiety issues since my teens but it's been worse this last year. I have a hard time opening up to anyone."

"Really?" His smile softened the sarcasm.

"Yes. When I woke up at your apartment and you offered me breakfast, the encounter turned into a date instead of a hookup. Dates weren't in my vocabulary, especially not with men, because I've been afraid of what my coming out as bi might do to my corporate reputation, but now . . ."

"Yes?"

"I'm not sure if I care. But before I can be comfortable coming out, I need you to know that my heart races every time I even imagine being in a real relationship, or having someone expect me to treat them decently, or know how to care for them. I'm working on it, but it's not going to change overnight, so if that's too much for you . . ." My chest tightened and I had to force myself to take a long, slow breath.

"Are you okay?" Nate asked.

"Yes, this is nothing compared to how I felt that morning at your apartment. I couldn't breathe, and I thought I would pass out. The last thing I wanted was for you to think I was a freak."

"Why would I—"

"It's not rational. Anxiety never is." I sighed. "Most of the time when I'm being a bastard it's because I'm afraid if I'm not abrasive, I'll simply break down."

"So you—"

I held up my hand, needing to finish. "I was an ass, but it was for the sake of self-preservation. I wanted to stay. I wanted to have pancakes with you. I wanted to go back to bed and fuck again but all I could do was run, because if I let you turn our time together into a date, I might have to open up to you more than I was capable of."

Nate laid a hand on my shoulder. "Thank you for explaining this to me now. And Adam?"

"Yes?"

"This isn't too much for me. You're not too much for me."

The tightness in my chest eased. "Really?"

Nate nodded. "Yes, really. Was this what you wanted to tell me after the meeting?"

"Sort of, though I might not have said it as well then."

Nate sighed. "I should've let you talk, but I was too pissed off that you'd made such an important decision without talking to me."

"I couldn't risk you wanting to talk me out of it."

Nate nodded. "I can see that."

"I didn't have any right to expect you to go out with me or to want what I wanted. I don't think about what others are feeling a lot of the time. I need to control things or I . . . fuck, I might fall apart."

"So what do we do now?"

"Eat dinner then maybe have a drink?" I held my breath.

"I like this dinner plan." Nate looked at the table again and smiled. "But I need to ask a question."

"Yes?"

"Do you want this to be a date?"

My heart pounded. I could say yes and nothing bad would happen. I knew that, but it didn't make it easy. "Y-yes."

"And if it goes well, would you consider going on another one tomorrow? One that takes place in public?"

"We went to dinner. That was in public."

"That could easily have been business. Hell, we more or less pretended it was."

"But it could have been something else."

"I don't want to be worried about how I'm going to react to you or that that I might say the wrong thing or I might touch you when we're in public. I want to know where we stand, what you're comfortable with now that I understand about your anxiety."

I looked away, willing him to accept what I could offer. "I don't think I'm ready for kissing you in public."

"Isn't it too late for that?"

My face heated as I thought of how risky our behavior at the club had been. "That wasn't . . . Okay, it was, but that's not the kind of kiss I mean."

"We could've been caught doing far worse than kissing, but you're right, it's different."

Deep breath. You can do this.

"I've known all along that getting involved with you would mean coming out. That's why I've fought it so hard. We can't hide this, not for long anyway."

"This?"

"What's going on with us."

"Which is?"

"I care about you Nate. A lot."

His face lit up. "Good. I care about you too."

"You don't hate me?"

"I've never hated you."

I looked away, my eyes tight and stinging. The last thing I was going to do was let Nate see me cry. "Someone at Kingston is going to see us together sooner or later if we do more than fuck occasionally. Our relationship will end up exposed."

"Are you ready to accept that?"

I thought for a few moments. Was I? "Yes, but I am worried about what people will say since we're running the company together."

"Couples run companies together all the time."

"True but—"

"Let me finish. I know that doesn't mean we won't get shit for it. I already have to deal with bigots who hate me just because I'm gay, and you're much more a public figure."

"You've had your share of publicity."

Nate sighed. "I have, and I don't want to make things even harder on you."

I shook my head. "I care about you, Nate. I'm no longer going to let any of this bullshit stop me from doing what I want. I asked you here, didn't I? And that was the scariest thing I've ever done."

"So I'm scary, am I?"

"Very."

He smiled.

I wanted to grab him, kiss him, shove his shorts down and suck him off, anything to revel in how good he made me feel.

"So you know how you try to live like you did before you were an executive and I . . . never have?" I asked.

Nate looked confused. "Yes."

"I want you to show me how to have fun like someone who doesn't have his own driver, someone who doesn't use money or power to manipulate people."

"I can do that. Tomorrow?"

I nodded. "It will also prove we can do something other than fuck."

"We did have one very nice dinner."

"And I thought about fucking you the whole time."

Nate laughed. "Did you now?"

"I did." I gave him a once over, and had to ask. "Do you wear them every day?"

"Panties?"

"Yes."

"Not *all* the time."

"What about at work?"

He grinned. "Occasionally."

"Right now?"

"Right now I'm not wearing anything."

"Fuck. I did not need to know that." Though my cock was very pleased with the knowledge.

"Enough about my underwear choices. Are you really saying you want me to take you for some normal Saturday evening fun?"

"I am." *I'll do this even if it kills me.* "But can you wear some underwear so I don't think about . . ."

"Blue? Pink? Yellow? You choose."

"Fuck, that's worse than commando."

"I thought it would be." Did he have to look so hot when he smirked at me?

"You really like tormenting me, don't you?"

He gave me a slow once-over. "I do." Then he took a step toward me and took my hand as his look turned more serious. "Are you sure you're okay with us being seen together?"

"I am. I'll restrain myself from making out with you in a restaurant, but if someone sees us and guesses we aren't just out as work colleagues then yes, I'm good with that."

Nate smiled. "Perfect. I know exactly where I'm going to take you."

"Where?'

"You'll find out tomorrow night."

I arrived at Nate's apartment in the late afternoon the next day. Once again he was wearing shorts, but this time his shirt was turquoise and short-sleeved. I'd left my suit jacket at home as a concession to dressing down.

"So how do you plan to introduce me to the world of normal dating?"

Nate studied him for a few moments before saying, "Let's go to Navy Pier."

"Are you serious? There will be tourists everywhere and it's crowded and—"

"You said you wanted to do something regular people think is fun."

"So Navy Pier?"

He nodded. "The Ferris wheel. Popcorn. Ice cream. Pizza."

"Pizza sounds good."

"And fireworks."

That not so much. "Let me guess. We're walking there."

"Of course, unless you'd rather bike."

"No." I glanced down at my suit. "I'm not properly dressed."

"There's not a dress code."

"But it's hot as hell."

He laughed. "Can't take the heat?"

"Why don't we stay here and fuck instead and I'll show you how much heat I can take."

"You're not getting out of this now. You can borrow some of my shorts and maybe my shoes. What size do you wear?"

I wasn't getting out of this. "Eleven."

"Perfect. So do I."

A bit later, wearing Nate's shoes and shorts, with the sleeves of my button-down rolled up, we headed out the door. Nate managed to flash the lace edge of his underwear as he dramatically bent over to pick up keys he certainly dropped on purpose.

I fought the urge to grab that lacy waistband. "I forgot to choose. I like that you wore the pink ones."

"They brought us together after all."

"Indeed they did."

On the walk to the pier, Nate pointed things out to me: street artists, food trucks, interesting architecture, a skateboarder with amazing abs, a pink wig, and bright yellow thigh high boots.

Did I really see so little of what was around me? Maybe that was why I'd been happy living in such a sterile space for so long. I'd never really paid attention, not until Nate. It was like seeing him in my apartment made me realize there was nothing of me for him to see. At first I thought that was great, but now, I thought it was kind of sad. So few people actually saw the real me. My father certainly never had. Valerie saw me. How the hell she pulled that off I've never understood. Apparently Nate had the same people-reading superpower. Maybe his skill could balance out the fact that I had next to no ability in that area. If someone wasn't yelling at me, crying, or jumping for joy, I rarely knew what they were feeling, and for the most part, I didn't give a fuck. At least I didn't use to.

When we reached Navy Pier, we made our way through the early evening crowds, which would surely grow thicker as the night went on. Nate looked longingly at a snow cone, and I offered to buy him one.

"Dinner first."

We walked by the outside tables for Giordano's, and I groaned in pleasure at the smell. "I'm starving."

Nate laughed as he paused near the entrance to the courtyard seating. "I love how you do that."

"What, starve?"

"No, react so viscerally to food. You try to be all objective and cold and logical, but when you're around food you love, your passion shows through."

"So let's get some, and you can expose me for the sensualist I am."

"You are one, you know. I'm very lucky that you show it around me."

I gave him a disdainful look. "You certainly are."

"Asshole."

"Treehugger."

We stepped up to the host station by the outdoor tables. "Two?" the host asked.

"Yes," Nate said. "How long is the wait?"

The host consulted his list. "About an hour and a half."

"What?" Was he serious?

"Pay no attention to him," Nate said, gesturing toward me. "He doesn't get out much."

I sputtered as Nate wrote his number down so the host could text us, then took me by the arm and pulled me away.

"I'm not waiting an hour and—"

"You said you wanted to have fun like normal people."

"No one thinks waiting for a table is fun."

Nate rolled his eyes. "No, but we can explore while we wait. We can sit by the lake and talk."

"We could get ice cream for an appetizer."

Nate laughed. "Maybe."

"But I'm starving."

"You'll live."

I glanced back toward the host stand. "I'm sure I could—"

"No, we aren't going to tell them who we are. We're going to wait like regular people."

I sighed.

"You've really never done this?" Nate asked as we starting walking along by the water.

"What? Walked around Navy Pier?"

"Waited for a table in a restaurant."

"No."

"Wow."

"Hush." I bumped shoulders with him. "So what do we do now?"

"We get tickets for the Ferris wheel, but we'll wait until after dark to ride it."

After we acquired our tickets, we went upstairs to the viewing area where people were watching the lake. Why they wanted to stand there staring at the water was beyond me. "Haven't they ever seen boats?" I asked Nate.

"Have you ever actually seen a boat yourself? Wait, let me clarify. One that's not a yacht where you've hired the captain?"

"Ha. I've seen cruise ships too."

"Canoes?"

I laughed. "Right. Me in a canoe. Can you see that?"

"One day I might."

"There's only so far I'll go to appease your desire to do normal things. And no, don't even ask about camping unless you mean staying in a three-star hotel."

"Never say never."

"I'm saying it."

"You probably said it about fucking me too."

He whispered the words but I still resisted the urge to look around and see if anyone had heard him. "Just shut up and show me whatever is next on the agenda."

"There's no set agenda. We're wandering Navy Pier having fun, waiting for pizza. Then when we're ready we'll ride the Ferris wheel and hang out until the fireworks."

"Fireworks?"

"Yes, you know. They explode in the air. They're a little loud. They happen after dark."

"In crowds."

Nate nodded. "Of regular people."

I huffed. "I suppose I'll survive."

"I promise, and if you're a good boy you'll get a nice reward."

I'd watch as many fireworks as necessary for another chance with Nate. How had I ever thought I hated him?

We studied the different types of boats on the lake and then went inside and marveled at the line at Garrett Popcorn. Fortunately Nate didn't make me stand in it and not long afterwards, our table was ready.

We ordered the meat lover's pizza and snickered over the name like we were twelve.

The pizza was fantastic, all Nate had talked it up to be. After we finished dinner, we walked some more to let our food digest and the evening to get darker. Nate insisted that riding the Ferris wheel with the lights on was a far superior experience.

"How many times have you been on it?" I asked.

"I don't know. A lot."

"Isn't it for tourists?"

"I love playing tourist. You miss so much of what is awesome about the city if you ignore all those attractions. Tell me you've been up to the Sky Deck."

I shook my head. "I live in a penthouse."

"One with a glass-floored balcony?"

I frowned. "No, but I suppose that could be arranged."

"Your building isn't nearly as tall either."

I pretended to consider that. "I could always try to buy the building and see if adding floors is structurally viable."

Nate rolled his eyes. "Now's probably not the best time to start a project like that."

"True, and it might be beyond even my reach."

"At least something is."

"You like me with limits?"

"Except in bed." He said it low, leaning close to me. Warmth spread down my body.

"We could go home now," I said. "We could always come here again to explore more."

"Nope, we're finishing this tonight."

"Bastard."

When darkness settled over the area, we got in the long line for the Ferris wheel. I was thankful we'd gotten our tickets earlier, but I wished there was a way around all this waiting.

"Isn't there like a pass or something for—"

"Rich men who are above waiting in line?"

"Well . . . Yes."

He shook his head. "You really are too much."

"Is all this delayed gratification supposed to make me a better person or something?"

"It should give you some perspective."

I wasn't ready to admit that it had, but despite all my complaints, the night had been one of the best I could remember. I would never have spent so much time exploring and watching the lake, the people, the shops if we hadn't had to wait for dinner.

When it was our turn to be loaded into a Ferris wheel car, I stepped in first. When the car wobbled, I sucked in my breath and tried to steady myself. I wasn't getting out, though. Surely it wouldn't be worse than a helicopter ride, and I'd handled those okay even if I hated them.

Nate sat next to me and moved close.

"You're antsy about this aren't you?" he asked as we began to move.

I glanced around the contraption we were in, trying not the think about why the seat was sticky. "I don't care for it but I'm doing it for you."

"You'll love the view."

"My apartment has a great view."

"This is different. And with everything lit up, it's magical."

View or no view, being pressed against Nate in the dark with the city laid out before us was magical.

We dropped down and then our car rose again. The lake shimmered, and the laughter and murmuring of the people below fell away as we soared up toward the night sky.

"Look." Nate pointed out over the lake. "You can see for miles."

I nodded.

"Amazing, right?"

"Yes, you are."

I could just see his grin in the dim light.

Eventually, the ride ended and we exited the car. After we'd walked past a few storefronts, Nate pointed to an ice cream stand. "You up for dessert now?"

"Yes!"

He gestured toward a bench someone was just vacating. "Wait there and I'll be back."

"You don't know what flavors I like."

"Trust me."

He returned with two cups of salted caramel.

I smiled at him. "I approve."

"I knew you would."

My ice cream began to melt as I watched Nate eating his, licking it from the spoon, slowly and carefully. He held my gaze as he did so, teasing me on purpose, and it was working all too well. I wanted his tongue on me.

"You shouldn't be allowed to eat ice cream when children are present."

"What?" He frowned as though perplexed. "Children love ice cream."

"I hope they don't like the obscene way you eat it."

"You mean this?" He looked right at me as he brought the spoon to his mouth. My gaze dropped to his lips. They were sexy as hell, even though he wasn't wearing any lipstick tonight. He sucked at the creamy-caramel-laced goodness, then swiped his tongue over the spoon to get any remaining drops.

"Fuck."

He laughed, clearly pleased with himself. "Later."

Before too long the fireworks started. I stood as close as I could get without putting my arm around him, though I wanted to. I also longed to sit in the grass with Nate on my lap, run my hands through his hair, feel the weight of him leaning against me, bury my face in his neck and breathe in his smell. Fuck, I was so messed up over him.

The familiar panic started to flutter in my chest. *Not now. Not when things are going so well.*

Nate must have sensed that something was wrong, because he turned to look at me. "Are you okay?"

"Yes . . . No."

He discreetly reached over to hold my hand. A person would have to study us carefully to notice in the dark. "Does this make it better or worse?"

"Better." I wouldn't have thought it would, but his touch anchored me. It made me able to think when all I'd felt before was the whirl of emotions, and the messages from my mind that told me to run.

I wasn't going to run though, not this time.

The fireworks banged and popped, reverberating in the night. We stopped trying to talk. My mind didn't actually go still, but it came as close as it ever did. I squeezed Nate's hand, and he gazed at me.

"Thanks," I said. "This is perfect."

Nate smiled softly. "Yes, it is."

Chapter
SEVENTEEN

We walked back through the crowds that poured out of the park after the fireworks ended. Families with little kids up way past their bedtimes, older couples, a group of tourists speaking French, another speaking Korean. I typically hated crowds but this was different. It felt right to be walking with the people of this city I professed to enjoy but rarely paid attention to. I liked walking in the dark, Nate beside me, the warmth of the summer night around us.

When we reached his building, he looked at me. "Do you want to come up?"

"Is that a joke?"

"No, I want to make sure this is really what you want, because from now on it's not just going to be a series of hookups. It's no longer just working our anger out on each others' asses."

I groaned. "Are we having another relationship talk?"

"We are."

"I avoided these for thirty-three years and now I have two in twenty-four hours."

"Well all good runs must come to an end sometime. If you choose to head home now I understand. This isn't going to be easy."

"Nothing with me is easy; ask anyone who knows me." He smiled. And I took his hands, there on the street in front of his building. "I'm no good at reading people or talking about how I feel—sometimes I don't know what I feel. But I missed you when we stopped talking. A lot. I want to see where this goes and right now I want to go up to your apartment and fuck."

"Yes, the latter part I could guess, but what happens if you don't like the choice you made afterwards?"

"Um . . . I tell you I'm freaking out, and you comfort me with a blowjob and more pizza."

Nate scowled at me, but he was obviously trying not to laugh. "At least that's a better plan than running. And seriously, tell me if you need to leave. As long as I know what you're trying to work through, we'll be fine."

"Maybe one day, I'll stop panicking."

"If not we'll figure out how to deal with it."

"Why?"

He frowned. "So you're comfortable."

"No, I mean why are you willing to put up with me?"

"Masochism?" I glared at him, but he smiled and squeezed my hand. "I like you. I just genuinely enjoy getting to spend time with the real you, even when that you is being an utter ass or when you're uncertain. But most of all when you are raw and uncontrolled."

Mmm. Raw and uncontrolled sounded perfect. "Then take me the fuck upstairs and make me lose control."

When Nate closed the door of his apartment, I leaned on it and studied him. I knew what I wanted. Would he do it? "I want to watch you jerk off."

Nate's eyes widened. "Really?"

"Yeah, I . . ."

"You're into that?"

"I am, but if you're not comfortable or something or . . ."

He grabbed a chair from the kitchen table and spun it around. "Sit there, put your hands around the edge of the seat, and don't move."

Fucking fuck, this was truly happening. He pulled off his T-shirt and then worked his way out of his shoes, socks, and shorts until he was standing in front of me in his pink panties.

"Don't take those off," I said.

He smiled. "I wasn't going to."

First he simply ran his hand over his cock, which was hard enough to push past the top of the panties. The way it strained against the thin lace was so fucking erotic.

"When did you first start wearing these?" I asked.

"You're fucking with my concentration." He stepped closer, until I could've leaned forward and licked his cock.

In an effort to stay focused and to frustrate him, I said, "Tell me."

He pushed the panties down in front just enough to free his cock and stroke it. "Later."

With his cock inches from my face, I no longer cared. I watched his hand moving up and down, slow for a bit and then faster. Then I looked up, needing to see his expression. He was watching me, his tongue visible between his lips, his eyes wide, a darker blue than usual.

"So fucking hot."

He increased the pace, and I dropped my gaze to his cock again, realizing that asking to watch had been a terrible idea. I wanted to touch, to taste.

I started unbuttoning my shirt, expecting him to admonish me, but he didn't. I pulled it off and tossed it on the floor. "I want you to come all over me."

"Holy fuck!" His rhythm faltered for a moment, but then he stepped even closer. My heart sped up, and I fought the urge to lean forward and take him in my mouth. I'd regret giving up the chance to live out my fantasy. Nate's eyes were closed now. He rolled his balls with his other hand, toying with them. I took hold of the chair again to stop myself from helping him.

"You're close, aren't you?" I barely got the words out between ragged breaths.

"Yes!" He was flushed now, color creeping up his neck into his face. His cock looked painfully hard, pre-come beaded on the tip, and he used it to slick up the shaft. "Adam! Fuck, Adam! Going to fucking cover you in come."

"Yes!"

He shot then, on my chest and neck and then right on my face. His spunk hit my cheek and I gasped. My cock jerked against my shorts—Nate's shorts.

He groaned. "So damn hot."

I wiped my eyes, but he'd managed to aim well. When I looked up, he was watching me like a predator. "Don't move. I want to clean you up."

His words made me shudder and he licked my cheek. "Has anyone else ever done this to you?"

"N-no."

"You like it?"

"Fuck," I groaned.

"I'll take that as a yes."

I needed more of his tongue on me. "Clean me up."

"Oh, I intend to, baby."

I shuddered, loving that he called me that just like I had before.

"Mmm. You like that word, don't you."

I nodded as he licked the other side of my face and then moved down my neck and my torso. He unfastened the shorts I'd borrowed and pulled down my briefs. My cock practically sprang into his hands, and I sank my teeth into my bottom lip as he slid his hand up and down.

"Can't last. Nearly came in my pants," I gasped.

Then he kissed the tip of my shaft and I jerked against him.

"You don't have to last. I'm still hungry."

"Holy fuck, could you be any hotter?"

He laughed around my shaft as he took it into his mouth.

"That's it. Oh God! Yes!" I slid my hands into his hair and fought the urge to force myself deeper. I wanted rough and nasty, but I also wanted him to take the lead. Unable to hold completely still, I worked my hips as much as I could sitting down, and he took more, making no protest.

I gripped him tighter and he groaned, the sound vibrating down my cock.

"Oh, fuck!" I was tugging on his hair, trying to thrust as he sucked harder, moved faster, did unspeakable things. His mouth was amazing. In moments my whole body tensed. "Nate, I . . . I can't—" I never got the words of warning out because suddenly I was coming,

When I'd wrung myself out, I opened my eyes and looked down. He let my cock slip from his mouth and licked his lips.

"Kiss me," I gasped. He rose to his feet, taking my hands and pulling me with him. I wobbled, dizzy from so much pleasure. When we kissed, I tasted both of us on his tongue, and the kiss deepened, turning fierce despite our exhaustion.

Seconds later, he pulled back so we could get our breath, he said, "College."

"What?"

"You asked when I started wearing panties. It was in college."

"Oh."

"I'd fantasized about it for years before that. I don't know where it came from. I'd masturbate to the thought of lace over my hand as I worked my cock. Lace and satin against my ass was just something my brain found sexy. Then I started seeking out porn where guys were wearing lingerie. It turned me on, but it wasn't as good as thoughts of it on me."

"I like it on you best too."

He laughed. "I've already had that impression. A year or so later, I finally worked up the nerve to order some for myself. I was nervous the whole day the first time I wore them, nervous and hiding a hard-on. I jerked off three times that night."

"Mmmm. I can imagine it."

"I bet you can."

"Come on." He took my hand and led me toward the bedroom.

"I may be pretty damn amazing, but I'm not ready to go again just yet."

Nate laughed. "Something the incredible Adam Kingston can't do? How can that be?"

I scowled, but he simply flopped onto the bed and patted the spot next to him. "Lay down and talk to me."

I tensed. Chatting side by side after sex was far from my comfort zone.

"Come on. I could give you another massage."

His hands had felt so good. "Okay."

I lay on my stomach and he straddled me, making me groan as he dug his fingers into my tense shoulders. "Is this okay?"

"Yes. Definitely yes."

He worked my neck, shoulders, and back until I felt like I might ooze right into the mattress. "When did you know you liked men?"

The question sounded far away. I was half asleep, in a post-sex, post-massage trance. "What?"

"When did you know you were bi?" Nate shifted position, stretching out beside me.

"High school, but I never really admitted it to myself until after college."

"Yeah?"

"Yeah, I told myself I was imagining that attraction, that I just found some men good looking, but I didn't actually want to sleep with them."

"Turned out you did, huh?"

"Yes. Yes, I did."

We both laughed.

"So you've never had a relationship with a man?"

"I've never had a relationship with a woman either unless you count Valerie, but we never had sex and only pretended to date."

Nate shook his head. "That doesn't count—not because of the sex, but because of the pretense."

"I love her, but not like—" I froze horrified. My stomach flip-flopped I'd almost said. *Like you.*

Nate's eyes were wide.

My mind screamed for me to run.

He reached for me before I could spiral too far into panic. "I feel it too. We don't have to talk about it anymore now, though."

"I didn't mean to . . ."

He smiled. "I know, but it makes me happy. You make me happy."

"How did we get here?"

"Well, we walked home from Navy Pier and—"

"Shut up."

He rolled his eyes.

"Can we just go back to me being bi?"

Nate nodded.

"Once I realized how much I liked it, I fucked men in secret and no one figured it out. Not even Valerie, until you."

"That seems so hard to believe."

"What part of it?"

"Valerie for one thing, but really just the fact that no one noticed. You've not been very discreet with me."

"My brain stops functioning when I look at you."

"We should probably get that under control."

I laughed. "Yes, we should or working together is going to be hell."

"If I have to watch you prance around in your perfectly-fitted suits, it's already going to be hard."

I glared at him. "There is no excuse for that."

He rolled over on his stomach. My gaze followed the line of his back down to his ass, which was still covered in pink lace.

"When did you realize you liked men in panties?" he asked.

"When I saw yours in your office."

"Seriously? You'd never been interested before? Because you were really fucking interested from the moment you saw them in my hand."

"So you did notice?"

"Oh, yes."

"I'd been intrigued by guys in lipstick, then told myself it was just because they looked ridiculous. But lingerie had never even been on my radar. I've always loved guys with muscular arms like you, with your height—"

"But not my manties."

"No, but when I saw you with them and thought about the contrast between your body and pink lace . . . I tried to tell myself that it wasn't sexy, that it was ludicrous, not something I'd ever like. Then I tracked you down that night and . . ."

"You liked it."

"A lot. But wanting you, that didn't start with the lace."

Nate smiled indulgently. "I know."

I rose on my elbow and let my fingers follow my gaze. I ran them under the waistband of his underwear, sliding along his smooth skin, teasing the top of his crack.

He looked up at me. "You ready now?"

I hadn't even realized how provocative my caresses had become. I just loved the feel of him. "Sadly, all I'm ready for is going to sleep."

"You want to stay the night?"

I nodded. "I do."

"And wake up and have breakfast?"

"Yes, please. I'd love another chance at pancakes."

He rolled to his side and reached for me. I scooted into his arms and sighed as I closed my eyes, content to be held.

Chapter EIGHTEEN

*J*woke from the first refreshing sleep I'd had in a long time and turned over to stretch. When my foot hit a man's leg, I startled.

"Good morning," Nate said.

"Hi." My heart sped up, but I wasn't going to let that deter me. *I'm fine. I'm staying.*

"Dare I suggest breakfast?" Nate asked.

"Yes, this time I'm staying put. But I need to shower first. I'm all sticky from last night."

Nate laughed. "We both are. Let's shower together. I'll get you squeaky clean, so I can make you filthy all over again."

"When I'm with you I don't know how to be anything but filthy."

He grinned. "I've noticed."

"This'll be another new one for me. I've never showered with someone I fucked." It was too intimate, too much about someone else in space that needed to be mine. Somehow it was okay that they'd been up my ass, but . . .

Nate smiled. "Ready to try something new?"

"With you I always am."

"I love that I can make you try new things, but that doesn't mean I want to change who you are. I happen to like you as an arrogant shit."

I smiled at him. "Who wouldn't?"

He slapped my ass and pushed me toward the bathroom. "Come on."

As Nate reached to turn the water on, he was already semi-hard. If I got on my knees I could suck him until he was ready to fuck me, but he wanted to shower with me so I restrained myself. I was going to let him seduce me into further intimacy if it killed me, though waiting to take his cock in my mouth again just might.

He pushed the pink lace he had still been wearing down his legs and tossed them into the laundry hamper. When the water was hot he stepped in, and I followed.

"Here." He handed me a container of shower gel. "I'll wash my hair while you get my body nice and clean."

I did like the idea of running soapy hands all over him so I squeezed some of the gel into my hand and started at his shoulders. I worked my way down his chest and then rubbed soapy circles on his back, lower and lower until I was sliding a hand into his crack and teasing his hole.

He encouraged me, "Go on, make sure I'm clean everywhere."

I pushed into him and he gasped as he ducked under the water to rinse. Liking his response, I pushed deeper until I brushed his sweet spot.

"Fuck," Nate sputtered, having sucked in water.

"Relax and enjoy this." I added more soap and slicked up his cock. By the time his shaft and balls were clean, he was fully hard, but I wasn't ready to do anything about that yet, so I worked my way down to his feet, planted a kiss on his ass cheek, and stood.

"Now it's your turn. Turn around."

I tried to take the shampoo from his hand. "I can do my hair."

"No, you get the full treatment."

I sighed. "Fine."

He pulled me back into the spray, getting my hair good and wet before he worked the shampoo through it, massaging my scalp with his fingers. It felt divine.

When he'd rinsed the shampoo away, he lathered up his hands with soap. "I think you need to be as thoroughly cleaned as I was, don't you?"

"I— Yeah, I do."

He moved to stand in front of me, wet skin sliding against mine. He washed my chest and then knelt. His face was so close to my cock as he thoroughly washed my balls and the creases at the top of my thighs that I lost the ability to breathe.

"Spread your legs."

I did. Why was it so easy to do exactly what he said?

He slipped his hand behind my balls, making soap-slick circles on my taint and teasing the edge of my hole.

I swore I wouldn't whine or whimper or otherwise embarrass myself, but as if he knew what I was thinking, he looked up and grinned in challenge.

He added more soap to his hands and massaged my ass cheeks. Then when he had me thoroughly relaxed, he slid his hands back down my crack and pushed a finger inside me.

I whimpered.

Nate groaned. "God, I love that sound."

"I fucking hate it."

He pushed deeper, and I made it again.

"You're incredible."

He worked his finger inside me, making me squirm. His mouth was less than an inch from the tip of my cock. I wanted to feed it to him. Instead, I squeezed his shoulders hard. Needing to touch, to do something, but suddenly he stopped and stood.

I stared at him. "Why are you—"

He grabbed me, shoving me again the wall of the shower, kissing me like he was starving.

"Fuck," I moaned as he kissed the line of my jaw. Then he sucked on my lower lip, and began to work our cocks together where they jutted up between our bodies. Just as I was getting into the rhythm, he stopped, jerking away.

"Not in here," he gasped as he reached behind me and shut off the water.

I was so eager, I nearly fell trying to get out of the shower, pulling him with me. I was headed to the bedroom but he caught me around the waist and spun me to face the mirror. "Brace yourself," he ordered.

My cock got impossibly harder. It was like the last time at the club, but this time there wasn't anger between us, only lust and whatever tension was always there under the surface, driving us to push each other. I looked up, catching his gaze in the mirror. He was so intent, so fucking hot. So not at all the man I'd thought he was.

"Stop fucking analyzing this," he demanded.

"It's what I do."

He grabbed a bottle of lotion from the counter and pumped some into his hand.

When he pushed two slick fingers inside me, I let my head drop, enjoying the stretching sensations as he shoved the digits into me hard and fast, and then oh-so slowly. I worked my hips, needing friction, needing more.

"Fuck me now!"

He laughed. "That's what I wanted, your mind on your ass and what I can do to it."

"Bastard."

He pulled my cheeks apart and teased my entrance with the tip of his cock.

"Now!"

He started to push in and then pulled back looking shocked. "I . . . I need." He yanked open a drawer started shoving things around in it. He finally found a box of condoms and dumped the packets on the counter. "I didn't mean. I . . ."

Fuck. I hadn't thought of it either. I'd been ready to let him take me bareback—talk about increasing intimacy. I'd fantasized about letting some guy I'd just met take me like that, but I was nowhere near that reckless. With Nate, though . . .

I grabbed Nate's arm, stopping him from ripping the packet open. "How hot would that be Nate? To go without it?"

He glanced at me in the mirror again. "Adam?"

"I get tested regularly and I've never gone without before, never wanted anyone so badly that I'd forget. I'm a lot more careful than my reputation would suggest."

"With women too?"

I nodded.

"And you trust me?"

I nodded again.

Nate frowned. "I've never . . ."

"I have with girls when I was much younger but never with a man."

He tossed the condom onto the counter. "You're changing me too. I never make decisions like this on the fly, but I've been tested recently, so . . ."

"It's a calculated risk." Was I really going to talk him into this?

"Look at me," he demanded.

I did.

"You swear you want this, and you're not lying to me about any of it."

"Nate, I will stretch the truth as far as I need to for a business deal, but I would never lie to you about this. I'm not sure I could lie to *you* at this point."

He caressed my ass. "You want my bare cock in you? You want to feel my come filling your ass, dripping down your legs when I'm done?"

I sucked in my breath. "Fuck yesssss."

"You're going to whine for me, beg for it?"

"I'll do anything you want."

"Yes, you will. Now watch me."

I could never disobey that commanding tone he had, the one I'd heard so rarely before we'd fucked. Nate coerced everyone else with his charm.

He pulled me open again, like he had before, his fingers digging into my ass cheeks. His cock teased me and then he pushed in just a little. He worked me with teasing shallow thrusts, a fucking smirk on his face.

"Quit playing with me."

"Feels so good. So fucking hot around my cock."

I started to say something, but then he drove deep, making me cry out. He held himself there, letting me adjust. But I didn't want him to go easy on me. I wanted it to hurt. "More!"

I thought he'd argue, but he gave me exactly what I needed. Hard driving strokes. And it was so amazing. He was fucking me with nothing between us, just hot tight skin.

I reached back, wanting to feel his cock as he entered me. Nate slowed his strokes so I could trace my finger around my rim.

"Fuck yes, baby!" he shouted. "Slide your finger in with my cock. Do it!"

It burned to stretch just that much more, but it felt incredible. Talk about opening myself up to him. This was extreme intimacy and I was loving it. I watched Nate in the mirror. His eyes were huge, his face flushed. "You love this, don't you? Fucking me bare."

"Yes. So fucking tight, so good."

"You want to come in me, to fill me up?"

"Yes," he growled.

I slipped my finger free and gripped the counter. "Do it."

He took hold of my hips and fucked me mercilessly. I couldn't breathe. I couldn't do anything but watch him as he watched me. Panic rose. This was too much. He was too much. What was happening? What was he doing to me?

"So close," he moaned. "Baby, I want to feel you come."

He stroked my dick, and that damn word and the expression on his face did just as much to send me over as his touch did. He fucking loved this. He was so lost to it.

"Nate! Oh fuck!" My cock pulsed, shooting come onto his bathroom cabinets.

He followed me seconds later. I felt heat flood my ass. That and the throb of his cock dragged one more spasm from me before I dropped to my elbows on the counter, dizzy, knees weak.

He pulled out and braced himself on the counter, breathing harshly. I could feel his come sliding from my ass. It was dirty and so hot. Something I'd never thought I'd share with anyone. I wasn't scared by it though, I was happier than I'd been in a long time.

"Wow."

"Yeah. Wow."

Somehow we made our way to the bedroom, holding each other and weaving like drunks. We collapsed on the sheets.

I frowned. "We're filthier than we were before the shower."

"Who cares?" Nate laughed and pushed at my thigh. "Roll over."

I did.

"Hands and knees."

"I don't think—"

"I want to see it."

Oh my God. My cock twitched. "Don't make me hard again. You'll fucking kill me."

He laughed. "It would be a good death."

"The best."

I squeezed my ass a few times and felt more come run out. I stared at him over my shoulder, saw him *watching* me. "You're a dirty boy."

He grinned. "I am."

"You seem so innocent at work, as though all your passion goes into enviro tech. And there you are wearing manties and thinking about come dripping from a guy's ass."

"I do not think about that at work."

"Seriously? I think about it all the time."

Nate chuckled. "Well . . . only rarely."

I rolled back to my side he stretched out next to me. "That is without a doubt the best sex I've ever had."

Nate's mouth dropped open. "Wait. Say that again."

I raised my brows and held his gaze.

"You're seriously admitting it?"

"Yes." And it hadn't even been difficult.

He grinned, looking so very pleased. "Same for me. I wonder if we'll ever top it."

"I think our goal should be to try as hard as we can."

"But you said I'd kill you."

"We're not starting now."

"Okay. What about tomorrow?"

"I like that idea. A lot."

I spent the night with him, and the next day we came close to succeeding. I finally had to drag myself from his bed because I needed to go tell Valerie goodbye. She was heading to the airport that evening to fly home.

Nate walked me to the door once I was showered and dressed. "I'll miss you," I said.

"You'll see me tomorrow or tonight if you insist."

"I like that. I like . . . this. Intimacy isn't so bad after all."

Nate slapped my ass. "Go on. You know Valerie's dying to hear the juicy details."

"And wow do I have some, not that I kiss and tell."

Nate's laughter followed me down the hall.

Chapter
NINETEEN

*V*alerie was already seated when I arrived for our lunch date. I kissed her cheek and took a seat across from her.

"You look disgustingly happy. If he fucked you that well, I'm surprised you can walk."

An older woman at a nearby table gasped and glared at Valerie.

Valerie smiled sweetly and said, "I see you're admiring my appetizer. I ordered the lobster nachos. They are divine. Highly recommended."

The woman sputtered and turned around.

God, I loved Valerie.

"I am quite happy, thank you," I said in my best prim and proper voice.

She rolled her eyes. "So what's up with you two now? Are you official?"

"We're more than fuck buddies if that is what you mean."

"So you're finally ready to admit it?"

I nodded.

"And if other people find out?"

"Fuck 'em."

She studied me intently. "Are you actually Adam Kingston?"

"I'm not even sure anymore."

"Well, I like this man who's sitting with me, so I'm going to pretend it's Adam and keep being friends with him."

"Good." I hesitated a moment. "If you hadn't pushed me toward Nate . . ."

She smiled and laid her hand over mine. "I'm truly happy for you."

"I have no idea how to have a relationship."

She tilted her head and looked at me. "You love him, don't you?"

Heat filled my cheeks. "Yes."

"Then you'll figure it out."

"But what if I don't? What if I screw it up? I don't do people well."

She gestured between us. "We work. Nate sees through you like I do. Just talk to him instead of being so fucking stubborn."

A waiter approached the table then. He refreshed our water glasses and then took our orders. Once he was gone, I said, "I almost told him."

"Told him what?"

"That I love him."

Valerie's eyes widened. "Holy shit."

"And he knew what I was about to say."

She made a circling gesture with her hand. "So—"

"He basically said he felt the same."

"Oh, Adam. You must have been terrified."

I nodded. "I was, but I'm also kind of excited. I think I might be ready to say it for real now."

Valerie grabbed my hand and squeezed it. "This is a big step for you and I'm proud of you for taking it. Don't worry too much about the future. You're Adam Kingston. You can do anything."

"Of course, I'm a fucking genius."

She laughed. "Now that's the man I know."

We talked a little more about Nate and then she told me about some of the shows she'd seen while she was in town. When it was time to say goodbye, I drew her into a hug before opening her car door.

She beamed at me. "Adam, you really have changed."

"I know. Fucking Nate."

"It's good. I'll be in New York at Christmas, but I want you to come see me before that."

"I think *we* just might."

She laughed and climbed into the car. "It's so good to see you finally figuring out how to have fun."

"Bitch."

"Asshole."

"Have a good flight."

She blew me a kiss and the car drove off.

I pulled out my phone and texted Nate. *You want to go to Nazapoli this fall? We could stay in a castle.*

Nate: *How could I say no?*

Me*: You can't.*

Monday mornings I usually forced myself through a long run and then got to the office by 7 a.m., ready to browbeat non-performers, make demands, and then forget all my meetings while tinkering in the lab, running experiments, or pouring over data.

This week was going to be a whole lot different.

I did the run. If I was going to keep up with Nate I had to stay in shape, but on the way in, I picked up a coffee and an herbal tea (fucking hippie) and two cinnamon rolls (at least he didn't expect those to be gluten free, dairy free or taste free).

I didn't head straight to my office. I didn't grill Brad on what was on the agenda for the day. I didn't even check to see if Brad had beaten me there. I'm sure he had, since it was now after eight. I went straight to Nate's office—well to the CEO's office—which I was hoping he'd moved into like he'd planned. I walked past his secretary, not slowing down when she tried to stop me—some things weren't going to change. He was there, looking out the window as if a little lost.

"I thought I'd try to get in good with the boss, so I brought cinnamon rolls."

Nate turned around and lit up with a smile. "I do not accept bribes."

"I have other things to bribe you with."

He stared down his nose at me. "I am a man of integrity."

I slapped the bag into his hand. "Eat your damn cinnamon roll."

"You want to sit?" he asked.

I set the coffee and tea down on the desk and settled into one of the chairs facing it. They were damn comfortable chairs. My father had always insisted on the best.

"This is so strange," Nate said.

I nodded as I pushed his cup toward him. "I got tea for you. No caffeine or anything."

"Thank you."

"I wanted to welcome you to your new position. Can we have a toast with hot beverages? It seems a little early for a cocktail, although some Irish coffee might not be amiss."

"Stop babbling," Nate admonished. Then bit into the cinnamon bun and groaned.

"Good, aren't they?"

"I take back what I said about not taking them as a bribe."

I laughed and then leaned back in my chair and closed my eyes as the enormity of this day hit me.

"This has got to be hard for you."

I sat up and glanced around at the office. I'd thought being there would remind me of what I'd given up, but all I felt was relief. "I did expect that this would be mine, but that's not what's bothering me. I'm truly okay with you being here."

"Yeah?"

I nodded.

"So what is it?"

"All of the sudden it's very, very real to me that my father is gone."

Nate didn't spit out some sympathetic platitude like a lot of people would. He also didn't reach for me, which was a relief. Not hiding was one thing. Touching each other in the CEO's office was something else.

"I know there are so many things the two of you didn't say to each other, but I think he'd be proud of the changes you've made in a short time, and while he might not—okay, definitely wouldn't—approve of us being together, he'd be glad to see you happy. He did want that."

I nodded. I'd re-read my father's letter countless times, and when I'd finally learned to read between the words and recognize all the things still unsaid, I'd seen that message: Let yourself be happy.

I looked at Nate, willing him to believe what I was about to say. "I really want this to work."

"Kingston Corp. or you and me?"

"Both."

He smiled. "Me too."

"I don't want you to see anyone else."

"I wasn't planning to."

"So this is it?" I asked. "We're in a relationship?"

He laughed. "Planning to change your Facebook status?"

"Not quite yet, but Nate?"

"Yes?" His eyes widened as if he sensed the seriousness of what I was about to say.

"I love you."

He gave me the most beautiful smile. "I love you too."

"Good." I picked up a remote from my fath—Nate's desk that allowed me to lower privacy screens on the windows.

"I didn't know they did that."

"My father believed in lots of perks. But I don't want to think about him now."

"No?"

"I want you to kiss me." I was already over the idea of not making out at the office.

Nate moved around the desk and leaned over me. He cupped my face and bent down until his lips almost touched mine. "Maybe we should take a lunch break."

"It's 9 a.m."

"Second breakfast?"

"Mmm," Nate said. "My favorite meal."

He kissed me then, his lips soft, barely brushing mine, the kind of kiss I wouldn't have imagined longing for before I met the real Nate Thomas. I licked his bottom lip, enjoying how plump and soft it was.

As he deepened the kiss, I wrapped my arms around him and held him tight, reluctant to let go. I wanted us to succeed, and with him in my arms and his mouth on mine, it was easy to believe we could do anything.

Dear Reader,

Thank you for reading Silvia Violet's *Lace-Covered Compromise*!

We know your time is precious and you have many, many entertainment options, so it means a lot that you've chosen to spend your time reading. We really hope you enjoyed it.

We'd be honored if you'd consider posting a review—good or bad—on sites like **Amazon, Barnes & Noble, Kobo, Goodreads, Twitter, Facebook, Tumblr,** and your blog or website. We'd also be honored if you told your friends and family about this book. Word of mouth is a book's lifeblood!

For more information on upcoming releases, author interviews, blog tours, contests, giveaways, and more, please sign up for our weekly, spam-free newsletter and visit us around the web:

Newsletter: tinyurl.com/RiptideSignup
Twitter: twitter.com/RiptideBooks
Facebook: facebook.com/RiptidePublishing
Goodreads: tinyurl.com/RiptideOnGoodreads
Tumblr: riptidepublishing.tumblr.com

Thank you so much for Reading the Rainbow!

RiptidePublishing.com

Also by
SILVIA VIOLET

Revolutionary Temptation
Coming Clean
If Wishes Were Horses
Needing A Little Christmas
Astronomical
Meteor Strike
A Carnal Agreement
Shifter's Station
Wolf Caller

Fitting In
Fitting In
Sorting Out
Burning Up
Going Deep

Thorne and Dash
Professional Distance
Personal Entanglement
Perfect Alignment
Well-Tailored

Unexpected
Unexpected Rescue
Unexpected Trust
Unexpected Engagement

Law and Supernatural Order
Sex on the Hoof
Paws on Me
Dinner at Foxy's
Hoofin' It To The Altar

Wild R Farm
Finding Release
Arresting Love
Embracing Need
Taming Tristan
Willing Hands
Shifting Hearts
Wild R Christmas

About THE AUTHOR

Silvia Violet writes erotic romance in a variety of genres including paranormal, contemporary, and historical. She can be found haunting coffee shops looking for the darkest, strongest cup of coffee she can find. Once equipped with the needed fuel, she can happily sit for hours pounding away at her laptop. Silvia typically leaves home disguised as a suburban stay-at-home-mom, and other coffee shop patrons tend to ask her hilarious questions like "Do you write children's books?" She loves watching the looks on their faces when they learn what she's actually up to. When not writing, Silvia enjoys baking sinfully delicious treats, exploring new styles of cooking, and reading to her incorrigible offspring.

Website: silviaviolet.com
Newsletter: silviaviolet.com/newsletter
Facebook: facebook.com/silvia.violet
Twitter: twitter.com/Silvia_Violet
Pinterest: pinterest.com/silviaviolet
Instagram: instagram.com/silvia.violet

Enjoy more stories like *Lace-Covered Compromise* at RiptidePublishing.com!

Working It
ISBN: 978-1-62649-522-7

How the Cookie Crumbles
ISBN: 978-1-62649-389-6

Earn Bonus Bucks!

Earn 1 Bonus Buck for each dollar you spend. Find out how at RiptidePublishing.com/news/bonus-bucks.

Win Free Ebooks for a Year!

Pre-order coming soon titles directly through our site and you'll receive one entry into a drawing for a chance to win free books for a year! Get the details at RiptidePublishing.com/contests.

40800967R00103

Printed in Poland
by Amazon Fulfillment
Poland Sp. z o.o., Wrocław